UNDER T RADAR

by

Philomena Digings

Copyright © 2024

All rights reserved. No part of this book may be reproduced or transmitted in any form or by any means without written permission from the author.

ISBN: 9798871413951

https://www.wordsflypast.com

DEDICATION

To my dear husband, Roger Digings
for all his help and support.

Introduction

This is the third book in the Anna Kinsale series. It's 1967. Anna is now a Detective Sergeant working at Woodstone police station, on the Essex / East London border.

(1) Something Lurking in the Forest

'A lurking person or animal is waiting where he, she, or it cannot be seen, usually waiting to attack or do something bad'. (anon)

Mary Ryan hums happily to herself as she organises the contents of the picnic basket that she and her fiance Tom have brought with them to the forest. Tom has wandered off to find some sticks for a fire to cook sausages. Suddenly, there is a scream. It's primal. Mary shivers. The sound has a raw intensity to it that tells of urgency, of desperate need. Mary stops what she is doing and listens intently. Another scream. This time even more intense.

Mary stands up and cautiously walks in the direction of the scream. if someone is in trouble she has to help…..Where is Tom ? She calls out to him, but there is no reply.

Suddenly, Mary feels cold despite the warmth of the day. Only hours ago, the day had begun by presenting her with an open summer sky, birdsong and the expectation of her lover's embrace.The trees were welcoming with their hug of browns, a shelter of extended limbs, resting beneath foliage in green hues. Mary knew the forest from childhood. She saw it as a protective mother, the promise of holy sanctuary.

Now, the trees that had seemed to embrace the pair in their gnarled arms, have become her enemies. Monsters.

"Tom," she calls loudly. "Tom, are you mucking about. ? Please stop it. I'm scared."

No reply.

Mary knew that the 'People's Forest' also has a dark side. Her imagination begins to run wild with panic. A dense and large woodland such as Epping Forest is the perfect place to make things disappear. Like people. She remembers learning that through the years, the bodies of people have been found buried in the forest. Several murders have taken place here too.

"Tom !" She walks unsteadily further into the maze of trees. She thinks about the size of the Forest, comprising nearly 6,000 acres of ancient woodland straddling the border between London and Essex. The trees close in on her and now it's getting dark. Despite the day, the trees release the sounds of a plethora of nocturnal ghosts, who create shadows in the darkness.

Mary is crying now. Tears flowing down her cheeks. "Tom ! Tom ! Please answer me."

Nothing.

Mary tries to think about what to do next. Think positive, she tells herself. She is sure there must be other walkers and picnicers nearby. After all, this is a taste of the countryside for Londoners. All these meandering footpaths which seem so threatening at this moment, are there to be enjoyed. Like the welcoming clearings where it's possible to stop and rest, or, as Mary and Tom had planned, to have a picnic. Hikers prefer the deeper, less well used, areas of the Forest. Maybe one will appear here now and help her. Mary looks round frantically as she walks, searching left and right for another human being

Nothing. Noone.

Mary stops to call again, but all she can hear is the echo of her own voice. She knows it is widely believed that the spirit of Dirk Turpin haunts this forest. Maybe Turpin is unable to find rest. He's known to haunt part of the forest in a place known for paranormal activities. Mary looks around her. Could this be the place ?

Mary stops. Try and pull yourself together, she tells herself. Maybe she's walked away from Tom and he's calling her. Despite turning back to retrace her steps, Mary thinks of the number of murder victims that have been discovered in the forest. One woman was found dead in her car with the arrow of a crossbow in her head ! Only a few years ago, visitors to the forest claimed to have seen two figures on horseback emerging from a forest pond. They rode in the direction of the town of Epping, but disappeared in front of the eyes of the visitors ! Another pond, deep in the forest, is said to have drawn people to commit suicide in its dark waters. Legend says that 300 years ago, this pond was the scene of the tragic suicide of two young lovers. People have also reported being touched and even pushed by unseen hands in some parts of the forest. There are even claims of people hearing terrified, high-pitched screams in this area………………….. That's it, maybe the scream she heard was just a ghost.

Mary turns to make her way back to the place where she has left the picnic things. To keep her mind occupied, she tries to go through the events of the morning. She remembers how Tom had pulled up outside her family's suburban house, a red brick 1930s semi-detached property with a well-tended front garden. She had watched from the front door as Tom carefully parked his newly acquired car. A Ford Anglia. It was what he had saved for and his mum and dad had chipped in to help him as a 21st birthday present. She had watched him walking up the path to the front door. She remembers smiling as he had passed the banks of roses either side of the path, loved and carefully tended by Mary's father. On a whim, Tom had gently picked one pretty pink rose. He had smelt its lovely scent. When he had arrived at the door, he offered her the rose. Mary had taken it, smelt its delicate perfume and invited Tom inside. A picnic hamper was waiting on the floor of the hallway. Tom picked up the hamper as Mary called "Bye mum. Bye dad. See you later." With the rose pinned to her dress, the couple walked to the car, smiled at one another and set off. Thinking back now, it had all seemed so normal. Mary's heart is beating hard as if she had been running. Concentrate, she tells herself.

Half an hour after leaving, they had arrived at their destination. Tom had sped along the main road, showing off the power of his new vehicle. They had both laughed. On arrival, in nature's hug of ever open arms of brown, and the cosy canopy of greens, the pair had felt comfortable and protected. There was a welcoming spirit that called to them. There was something deep amongst the trees that they felt drawing them in. They had wandered further into the trees to seek out a private area away from families and any other signs of humanity. The place they had arrived at is known as

'The Fairy Path'. They wanted privacy. Just the two of them in this secret place. There seemed a softness to the forest floor, to the moss that supported their feet, then sprung back. The woodland was the birdsong, the playful light flickering through the trees and the serenity of time that flows there without the clocks which ruled their usual weekly routines.

After a time exploring, they had found a quiet place. No human voices. No childhood laughter. While Mary unpacked the picnic, Tom had gone off to find his twigs and small branches for the fire.

A waterfall of tears continues to fall down her cheeks. As Tom had walked away, Mary remembers sitting on the mat she had brought with her and humming happily to herself as she organised the contents of the picnic basket.

Suddenly, there was that awful scream. Mary shivers. That sound. Then another scream.

Mary's anxiety is mounting. She can feel it building like an electric storm in her brain, creating a painful headache.

"Tom. Tom, are you there ?"

Silence.

Then, as she reaches a more open area, panic strikes as suddenly, a sight slams itself into her brain. A shape lies motionless on the ground. She slowly approaches what appears to be a bloody mess on the forest floor. She turns away, looking back out of the corner of her eye, not wanting to take a further look. She forces herself foward.

"Tom," she calls. "Tom", but there is no response from the silent figure lying so still on the forest floor.

The breeze through the trees changes direction and allows more sunlight to shine on the sight in front of her. As she draws closer. what she can see is grotesque. She stares and notices eyes, blackening and swollen over. There is bloody spit drooling from slack jaws. Instinctively she takes a step backwards. A thought buzzes through her head that she should telephone for an ambulance. She can't quite believe that this is Tom. Her Tom. Reduced to such a gory corpse ? A dead creature. Mary freezes. Could there be a wild animal in the vicinity ? Is she in danger ? What can she do ? Get away. Yes, get away and maybe the nightmare will come to an end.

She listens intently, casting her eyes around, thinking she had seen the shadow of a monster disappearing into the sanctuary of the trees. Did she hear a rustling sound or was that her imagination ?

Firstly though, she kneels beside the body of what had so recently been her loved one. She can't bring herself to kiss the mutilated face, but she gently touches an arm. As she does so she hears a rustle in the trees. She looks up, terrified. She hears a sound. Heavy breathing. Without looking again, she runs as fast as she can back the way she had come, forcing one leg in front of the other. She ignores the picnic and the hamper and runs to the car park. She frantically scours the area for a telephone box. She hurries onto the main road. About 100 yards away is a familiar red box. She runs as fast as she can, wondering how she could make a call without money. As she enters the box, she remembers that you can dial 999 for emergencies free of charge. She picks up the receiver in her shaking hand and dials.

A friendly female voice speaks. "Which service do you require ?"

Mary can hardly open her mouth. Her whole body feels frozen to the spot. She forces herself to speak, noticing how the hand holding the receiver is shaking. "U'mm, police....and ambulance please." She knows in her heart an ambulance is unnecessary, but she asks for it anyway.

The lady at the end of the line asks for her location. Mary's mouth feels like it did when she had been to the dentist for a tooth out. Numb. She speaks in a garbled way and is relieved when the operator replies "I'll contact the police and send an ambulance. Just stay put," she adds quietly. "Was there anything else ?"

Mary wants to scream and explain it was all a hideous nightmare, but instead, she mutters "no thank you," and hangs up.

She makes her way back to the clearing and, absent-mindedly, for something to take her mind off the horror, she packs away the picnic things into the hamper. She sits, or rather collapses, onto the ground. Tears stream down her face. She feels drained. After what seemed like hours later,she listens to the approaching sirens growing louder.

A police car follows an ambulance into the parking area. A policeman leaves the car and runs over to the collapsed figure of Mary.

Mary doesn't look up. An ambulance man arrives. They clearly think she is the casualty.

"What's the problem ?" asks the ambulance man. "Are you injured ?"

Mary looks up at him, but cannot speak.

"I think she's in shock," the ambulance man explains to the police officer.

The police officer is young. He crouches down next to Mary and speaks gently. "Take your time. What's your name ?"

"Mary", replies a tiny, weak voice."Mary Ryan."

"What's happened, Mary ?" continues the policeman.

Mary raises her arm and weakly points to the group of trees from which she had recently emerged. She wished she could turn back time and set out the picnic things while Tom went off to find twigs. "In there. Past the trees……" Tears stream down her face. She can't speak again.

"The police officer speaks to the ambulance man. "Look, I'll go and take a butcher's. Hang on just a sec and then you can take her to hospital."

The ambulance man nods.

"No," screams Mary. "I can't leave him."

"Who's that ?" asks the police constable, now looking more worried.

"Tom." The sound of the word makes the tears fall more heavily.

"Has something happened to Tom ?"

"It killed him." Mary is adamant.

"It ?" queries the policeman.

"The monster ! The creature !" Mary is shaking.

"Tell you what, you go with this gentleman," suggests the police constable, pointing to the ambulance man,"and I'll go and see if I can find him."

The ambulance man places a blanket around Mary's shoulders and gently helps her up and takes her to the ambulance. He assists Mary as she climbs aboard. "Now you just wait here while the police officer goes to see what's what," he suggests.

Mary hangs her head low and does as she had been asked.

Moments later she catches the eye of the ambulance man and mutters, "he's dead you know. It killed him……the monster…." her voice trailed away.

The ambulance man gives his driver a questioning look and looks puzzled. He sits patiently with Mary while they wait.

A short while later, they watch in amazement as the police officer appears from the trees and dashes to his car. The ambulance driver strides over to the police car and listens as the young constable makes his report on the car radio.

"I'm in the clearing in Epping Forest known as Epping Green. I have one death to report and a young lady who needs to be taken to hospital. Her name is Mary Ryan. The ambulance is here. I'll let her go and maybe someone could go to Epping Hospital and see if they can get any more information from her as to the circumstances of the man's death. I need a search party, Scene of Crime Officers and the pathologist here as soon as possible."

The desk sergeant at the other end of the phone asks, "Any indication of cause of death ?"

The police constable, James 'Jim' Gibson, hesitates.

"Well spit it out lad," says the desk sergeant impatiently.

The response is totally unexpected. "Well, it looks as if....as though....the bloke has been attacked by a wild animal."

"Come on young Jimmy, don't muck about."

"I'm not," replies PC Gibson. "The injuries are horrible. Looks as if he's been badly savaged. Made me throw up if you want the truth."

"Bloody hell," exclaims Sergeant Barnes in a different tone. "I'll get a team onto it pronto. Stay put....and", he laughs in a lighter tone, "you'd better wait in the car. Don't want any more victims do we ?"

There is no reply.

---

(2) A New Adventure

"An adventure a day keeps the routine away." – Jon Miksis

At the end of her previous case, Anna had been given time off work to recover from its consequences: including her having been kidnapped by a vicious gang leader and held hostage. Anna knows that a positive attitude is essential in her job. She constantly reminds herself that positive thoughts relating to events and their outcomes can act as a catalyst for producing excellent results.

On Monday 8th May 1967, as a result of a successful verdict based on excellent police evidence, the trial judge sentenced the gangland Lydon brothers to life imprisonment with a recommendation that they serve a minimum of 30 years. The severity of the sentences reflected the seriousness of the crimes. The charges included the murders of Jack (Jacko) Sykes, Sheila Graham and her boyfriend.

Eddie Hill and his brother Charlie, received consecutive sentences which included being convicted of The White Swan Club affray, conspiracy to pervert the course of justice and inflicting grievous bodily harm with intent, including threatening behaviour with a deadly weapon. For Eddie, trying to avoid arrest was added. Eddie was sentenced to 12 years and his brother to 10 years.

One of the Hills' gang, Arthur Mower, who gleefully did anything that Charlie Hills directed, plus providing some inventive and vicious ideas of his own, was sent down for a total of 15 years. A potpourri of lesser members of the gang, were sentenced for a miscellany of lesser crimes. They received sentences varying from 5 years to 18 months.

The removal of the two Lydon brothers from the crime scene left a vacuum for criminality in North Essex and the East End of London. The same applied to the area south of the River where the Hills had held court. Some of the Lydon gang members had known, worked with, or clashed with the Hills. This combination of bits and pieces of criminality enabled both police forces to round up a number of peripheral figures in the world of crime. These figures had worked behind the shadow of the Lydon's combination of Johnny's business acumen, his brother's ferocity and their joint use of threat, torture and murder. It was a similar set-up in terms of Charlie Hill, the brains and Eddie Hill, the brawn.

The remarkable achievement by both the Essex and Metropolitan Police Forces was due to the dedicated band of detectives and uniformed officers working in unison. Frank Fernbank remained at Woodstone Police Station and was promoted to DCI (Detective Chief Inspector) Murray Jacobs became DI (Detective Inspector) and is now working for the Metropolitan Police Force (nicknamed 'The Met') at Stratford in East London. Anna Kinsale was promoted to DS (Detective Sergeant)and remains at Woodstone. PC Tom Bradley received a commendation for bravery award for his actions in rescuing Anna from her imprisonment.

Anna Kinsale and Murray Jacobs became an item after the case was completed. Anna is hoping that she will not be expected to resign if she gets married. That is common practice in many professions, including the police. Anna and Murray will now be working in different police stations, otherwise that would be considered an issue.

"Probably expect us to be snogging in the broom cupboard at every opportunity !" Murray had giggled.

Anna had laughed, but secretly she thought the whole idea of two professionals not being able to work together was daft. 'Hey-ho', she had said to herself. Old-fashioned ideas clung on despite a new generation of more enlightened young adults. Anna had no doubt, of course, that her parents would think the idea of being a married female police officer was ridiculous. Anna ensisaged her mother saying, "but when would you get all your household chores done, dear ?" Her dad was known to venture into the kitchen on occasions, but he was kept under strict supervision by her mum, who never believed that he could master even making a cup of tea ! Mum would usher him out like a naughty child up to mischief.

Even Anna's boss, DCI Frank Fernbank, thought it strange that Anna would want to keep up her job after marriage. He would see it as Murray's role, as husband, to protect Anna. How could he do that if she was running around catching criminals ? In his fifties, Frank Fernbank belonged to the same generation as Anna's parents. In both his private and professional life, he was 'Old School'.

Perhaps due to her modern thinking, Anna had not yet committed herself to a wedding date. The general consensus of both Anna's parents and her friends seemed to be that she'd caught her fish and should now reel him in before he escaped ! Even Murray was hinting at fixing the date ! Anna wanted to think carefully. It was a big step and she wanted to be sure. Some had suggested she was being awkward and should come to her senses and get on with it. The decision hung like a weight. Strange, because she did want to marry the love of her life. She did also want to keep her job which she loves. She knows she has to leave the starting line and get on with the race. For the present, now fully recovered from her kidnapping, DS Anna Kinsale is back on the job at Woodstone 'nick' and ready to take on her next case. DCI Frank Fernbank is still Anna's boss.

Since being fully recovered from her ordeal, Anna has not had a big case fall into her lap. Paperwork has been the order of the day. However, she had also been sent on a Drugs Awareness course. One of the reasons for this was that prior to the Lydon and Hills brothers being imprisoned, it had been noted countrywide by town and city police forces that drug dealing and usage was increasing alarmingly. During the investigation into the operations of the Lydon and Hills brothers, it was discovered that drug dealing had been a new and profitable element in their illegal business practises.

On her course, Anna had discovered that only in the previous 5 years, the use of LSD and other psychedelic drugs began to be advocated by emerging proponents of consciousness expansion such as Timothy Leary and others in the world of pop music and alternative arts. These and other drugs such as heroin and cocaine, were said to profoundly influence the thinking of a new generation of youth. The consequences of this was having a negative impact on health or functioning and, more dangerously, led to drug dependence. In turn, this was now proving to be part of a wider spectrum of problematic or harmful behaviour.

This bright Summer's day, Anna smiles to herself, thinking of the small office she had shared with her previous partner and the constant untidiness of Murray's desk and his special filing system. The latter involved making paper aeroplanes from memos sent from Central Command and aiming them at the waste paper basket which, inevitably, quickly became full and then over-flowing. When things got too bad, Anna would make half hearted attempts to clear the worst of it and restore it to Murray's inbox. She sometimes got cross with him, but today, the picture seems more like a pleasant memory. Anna sighs and begins reading more messages and filing them in grey box folders where many of them would rest until they finally got sent to the basement. This is an underground area full of boxes filed in month and year order and overseen by Sergeant Jack Hawkins. Some appear to date back to the days of the Magna Carta. Everyone in the nick reckons that Jack sleeps amongst his files so that nobody can access them without his permission.

Anna checks her watch. 12.30. Time for lunch, she tells herself. The 'nick' is lucky enough to have its own canteen. Midnight feasts and breakfasts are provided for those officers working night shifts, lunches for any officers on day duty, as well as meals for those involved on overtime when serious cases needed everyone present for as long as they were needed. There's a standing joke at Woodstone and other police stations where the environment of the canteen is said to be perfect for 'sausages and story-telling'. In fact, it's the place for camaraderie, exchanging ideas and giving and receiving advice. It's often where team-work is strengthened and advice offered. It could be said that the canteen acts as a place for unofficial, yet beneficial, training ! Sausage, chips and chat have often been known to move an investigation forward !

Anna knows that any, probably new recruit, who questioned the need for long stretches of overtime would get the same response from Frank Fernbank. "Leave now if you like, just don't bother to come back". At which, a red faced youngster would slink away, having learnt a lesson.

Anna reaches the canteen. A queue is forming. One young female PC asks what is for lunch.

Betty Higgins, a red-faced, rotund lady in charge of the canteen, smiles back. "Shepherd's pie, dear, or, if you prefer, shepherd's pie."

There is muted giggling amongst staff and customers. An embarrassed recruit holds out her plate. Betty plonks a helping of shepherd's pie onto the proffered plate. The young woman moves along and receives a splodge of what appears to be cabbage. The whole is then christened with thick, rich gravy. The young woman moves away to collect her cutlery from the shelves and sits down alone. Anna collects her meal and joins her.

"Mind if I sit here ?"

"No. No. Please do," is the shy response.

Anna puts down her tray on the table and holds out her hand. "DS Anna Kinsale."

"WPC Lily Saunders." The young woman smiles.

Anna settles herself and picks up her cutlery.

Lily looks admiringly at Anna. " DS. You must be very proud ?"

Anna nods. "It's new. I've been promoted recently from DC."

"I think I've heard about you. Didn't you get kidnapped by a gangster ?"

"Amongst other things, yes."

"It must have been very exciting," says Lily, sounding like a child meeting an adult role-model.

"That's one word for it," is the response.

"Sorry. I've got a big mouth," explains Lily apologetically.

"That's OK," responds Anna. "Water under the bridge, now."

They continue their meal. Anna finds out that Lily has only been in uniform for a month. She is 19 years old. Most of her time, Lily admits, has been spent making tea for the men and filing paperwork. Anna is still in her twenties, but this young woman seems so young, not much more than a child. Is that how she had been perceived by Frank and Murray at first ?

As they finish their meals and begin moving from the table, Anna says, "If I can help at all or you'd like some advice, feel free to speak with me."

Lily blushes. "Oh. Thanks a lot."

....

As Anna approaches the office, she notices a visitor waiting there. It's her boss, DCI Frank Fernbank.

"Ah, there you are Anna." Fernbank ushers Anna into her office and shuts the door. "We'll just wait for Roger."

Roger Edwards is a DI. He and Anna share their tiny office. Anna had been pleased to find that Roger, unlike Murray, is a tidy and meticulous person. No overflowing waste bins or paper aeroplanes ! In his mid-thirties, he is quiet and serious, but he is good at subtly taking charge of a situation. All that said, Anna misses Murray and his outgoing, mischievous personality. Mind you, as her fiance, it's probably best if they don't work together !

Roger has also got the job of giving out information to the press. A task that Frank Fernbank hates and had quickly lumbered Roger with. Roger didn't mind. He had been a grammar school boy, having passed his 11+. His parents had ideas for him to become a teacher or a doctor. They were puzzled and worried in equal measure when he chose a career in the police. He had taken some ribbing from his new colleagues when he had first arrived at Church Road nick because they thought he sounded 'posh'. However, he'd taken it in good humour and it wasn't long before he'd become just one of the lads. That had been 10 years before. Now, he was taking Frank Fernbank's place at Woodstone as DI, whilst Fernbank had been sent to Heaven – the first floor where senior staff had their offices and God, alias Chief Superintendent Victor Jenkins, resided.

Anna knows straight away that something is in the air.

Once she is in the room, Fernbank closes the door. "Well now, we've got a strange one here. Sergeant Barnes, has had a call from a police car…..a young 'plod' saying that he has discovered a body in Epping Forest. The Sergeant has sent the usual team to fence off the area and guard the scene until we get there. I want you two to go out there and see what's what."

Anna's heart gives a leap. Action at last !

" You should know that…." Fernbank examines his notebook. "A young man, Tom Preston, has apparently been killed by a wild animal and his girlfriend, one Mary Ryan, may have witnessed this.." Fernbank pauses.

Anna and Roger are all ears.

"Apparently, according to the PC who attended the scene, young Jim Gibson, he spoke to….." Fernbank consults his notebook...."Mary Ryan... the pair were going out for a picnic.....they had driven out to Epping Forest....I assume for a bit of 'how's yer father' "he smirks..

Roger and Anna exchange glances.

"They walked into the trees and found a clearing where they spread out their picnic. They had brought some sausages with the idea that Tom would collect some twigs and pieces of fallen branches and build a fire to cook the sausages on."

"Lighting fires in the forest is a criminal offence isn't it ?" asks Roger.

Frank Fernbank nods. "Anyhow, that's by the by now. Tom leaves Mary sorting out the picnic things." Fernbank's grin disappears as he explains, "before they could do anything else, someone or something appeared and attacked the lad.."

Fernbank pauses whilst his colleagues look baffled and then continues. " Mary hears a scream. She waits, but silence. Anyhow, after a short time she makes her way back to the place she thought the scream had come from. What does she find ? The mutilated carcass of her boyfriend lying in a pool of blood."

"God !" responds Anna.

"According to the constable, who also saw the body, he said it was hardly recognisable as human."

"Bloody hell !" exclaims Roger.

Anna is silent. This didn't make sense.

Roger speaks. "You're sure this isn't a windup Frank ?"

Fernbank shrugs his shoulders. "That's what I might have thought if PC Gibson hadn't reported it in... The 999 callout was from a phone box. Apparently, the young lady, Mary Ryan, gave the PC contact details of the lad's parents and her own before being taken to hospital suffering from shock. No other injuries though.I think you both should visit the scene of the attack. get as much info as you can. I'll speak to PC Gibson when he gets back to the station. I'll radio you if there's anything to pass on. Take two cars. Roger, When you've finished at the scene, I would like you to visit the Ryans to give them the news. They will probably want to go straight to the hospital. Follow them and try to get a statement from Mary Ryan. Anna, you go to the Preston's house and see the dead lad's parents."

The two detectives head out to their respective cars. When they arrive on the scene, the pathologist, known as 'The Doc ' is already there. The Doc, Richard Bevin, is a bald, rotund, middle-aged man with a seemingly jolly nature.

"Hello there you two. Taken your time, eh ?" He laughs loudly.

What've you got ?" asks Roger.

"Follow me."

The two detectives walk to the scene and stand back whilst the Doc points at what appear to be the remains of a wild animal attack.

He addresses Anna and Roger. "Quite frankly I'm baffled. It's true the poor chap appears to have been savagely attacked by a wild animal, but there are a few things that don't seem right."

Roger nods agreement. "It seems strange because I've never heard of any such animals being found in this area. Zoos and the like are duty bound to inform their local police station if such an animal had escaped."

The doc adds. "I think we'll get the remains back to the mortuary. When I've completed my examination more thoroughly I'll let you know what I think."

Plods are left to guard the scene and make sure that things are not disturbed whilst the doc and forensics have a closer look and report back later.

Anna and Roger leave the scene. They go their separate ways.

Anna drives to the Preston's house. A rather frumpy, middle-aged woman answers the door. Anna introduces herself and is invited in.

"Cup of tea, dear ?" asks the woman.

"No thank you. Would you like to sit down, Mrs Preston ?"

"What is it ?" asks the woman, already suspecting bad news and looking anxious.

"It's your son," says Anna gently.

"Tom ? Has he had an accident ? It's a new car you know. I've told him to be careful."

"No….it's not that…." Anna takes a deep breath and then speaks formally. "I'm so sorry to have to inform you that there has been an accident and Tom has died."

"Died !!" Mrs Preston screams loudly. "No, you've made a mistake, dear." Her words are garbled. "He and Mary…that's his fiancee, have gone to Epping Forest for a picnic. "It's such a lovely day…" She looks away from Anna and peers out of the window at the sun shining in a blue sky. "You must have it wrong." Mrs Preston looks pleadingly at Anna.

"I wish that was the case, but I'm afraid that Tom's fiancee reported the situation to the police officer who attended the scene."

Mrs Preston looks vague.

Anna knows that shock is that feeling of pause while the brain tries to make a new connection. When she had been held prisoner in an old warehouse, she remembers thinking that it was like finding yourself on a platform with a train approaching. She had to board the train, just like she was obliged to stay put as a prisoner. The destination was not a choice. In her case, she had been able to leave the train. For Mrs Preston she has to travel in a direction in which she doesn't want to go.

Mrs Preston begins to weep quietly. She is soon a very distressed woman, whose eyes have become red from weeping. She looks haunted.

"I'll make you a cup of tea," suggests Anna.

There is no reply. Anna stands and moves over to the sofa where Mrs Preston is sitting like a crumpled Guy Fawkes dummy. Anna sits down next to her and puts her arm around her shoulder. "Can I phone someone ? Your husband ?"

Mrs Preston retrieves a hanky from her pocket and wipes her eyes. She looks at the clock on the mantelpiece. "He should be home anytime now."

Anna heads for the kitchen and makes tea as quickly as she can. When she returns with the tea she hands a cup and saucer to Mrs Preston, who like an automaton sips her drink.

Anna holds her cup and saucer, watching Mrs Preston. "What's your first name, Mrs Preston ?"

A hint of a smile looks at her. "It's Elsie dear."

"I'm Anna", replies the young detective.

....

Back at Woodstone 'nick', Fernbank is sitting at his desk. He picks up the telephone receiver and dials a number. A man answers the call. The DCI introduces himself. The man is Peter Ryan, Mary's father. He identifies himself.

DCI Fernbank relates the dreadful news as calmly and gently as he can.

"My wife and I will go to the hospital immediately," Peter Ryan says in a halting voice.

" My colleague, Detective Inspector Edwards is on his way to your home to explain. I will ask him to go directly to the hospital. Ask him to let me know when Mary wakes up," instructs DCI Fernbank. "If and when she's able to be released, I'll send a WPC to your home to ask some questions. Better than dragging her down to the station in such a state."

Peter Ryan whispers a quiet thank you. The DCI says goodbye to Mr Ryan and hangs up.

DCI Roger Edwards heads straight to the local hospital where Mary Ryan is being treated. He has received a radio call from DCI Fernbank to inform him that Mary's parents are now en route to the hospital. When he arrives, he is directed to the room where Mary is recovering. Her parents are already there. Roger identifies himself and they exchange greetings.

After a short pause, Peter Ryan explains to Roger, "It sounds crazy, but Mary's sure that she saw, or thought she saw, some kind of wild animal. She even suggested a wolf. I thought it was just her imagination trying to make sense of what happened. But from what she told us about Tom's injuries, it could be possible....I thought I'd better mention it to you anyway." His voice trails away as emotion takes hold.

Roger is puzzled, but in his long experience in the police force, things that seem impossible could well be true.

---

(3) The Plot Thickens

"When the primitive brain takes over, when the prefrontal cortex is switched off, primitive things happen with permanent consequences, with lasting pain and lasting damage." (anon)

Anna and Roger both return to the station and report back to DCI Fernbank. Anna suggests she could ring round zoos to see if any wild animals had escaped. Roger adds that he'll contact the University of London and see if they have a zoologist on the staff who might be able to throw some light on the subject.

Mary Ryan had been diagnosed with shock and released into her parents' care. She had returned home with some medication. Her parents had been told to take her back to the hospital if any other symptons appeared. DCI Frank Fernbank explains that he has given WPC Saunders the task of visiting the girlfriend, Mary Ryan. He hopes a young lady of a similar age might make Mary feel less threatened and, in that case, she might open up more. It is a big responsibility for the young WPC. However Anna agrees that she is a good choice. Privately, she thinks that Lily Saunders deserves the challenge and is confident that she will discover more useful information to help solve this mystery.

The following morning the investigation team is hard at work with their respective tasks. The DCI has scheduled a meeting after lunch to see what progress has been made. The doc has promised that a report of his initial findings would be available by lunchtime.

At 2pm sharp, everyone assembles for the meeting.

DCI Fernbank begins. "I have received a report from WPC Saunders concerning her visit to the home of Mary Ryan, the girlfriend of the deceased and the only witness as to what did occur. When I spoke with Mr Ryan, the father of Mary Ryan, he was of the opinion that Mary had actually witnessed the attack. However, things are less clear now. It seems that the couple had taken some sausages with them. The intention was to light a fire, and cook the sausages over the fire. "

There are muted sniggers at this information from some of the more junior staff. DCI Fernbank stops this with an intimidating stare.

The DCI continues with the briefing. "While Mary was sorting out the contents of the picnic basket, Tom had wandered off to gather some wood for the fire. Mary has explained to her parents that she heard a terrible scream. She hurried in the direction that Tom had taken to see if she could help. It was then that she thought she saw a strange animal-like figure disappearing into the trees. She says it had grey fur and appeared bigger than a large dog. That's how she came to believe it was a wolf. However, she only saw it for a split second in the shade of the trees. She was terrified. Her first instinct was to see if Tom was injured, but when she examined him she realised that the wounds he had suffered were too serious to give her any hope that he was alive. She instinctively made a run for it, fearing the creature might return. She ran back and waited in the car. After a time, when she could see and hear nothing more, she pulled herself together enough to realise that she had to call for help."

"There's doubt about the wolf idea," says Roger. "That ties in with my findings so far. I've asked round local zoos, even rang London Zoo. They all say either they don't have wolves and, even if they did, they would have to report it to the authorities if one had gone missing. There is a zoologist at the University of London. Dan Rivers. I spoke to him and he says that it would be unlikely to find a wolf in the forest so close to London, other than an escaped one, because of the proximity to town and people and the limited size of the forest. He also explained that wolves are pack animals and a lone wild wolf would be highly unlikely in that situation. He also said that Wolves tend to be more predatory - in that they use stealth and teamwork as well as the element of surprise to take down their prey, giving it almost no opportunity to escape.

But in terms of aggression to defend a particular place, wolves would only do that if their food or the well being of their pack or of pack-members is at stake. Roger goes on to explain that Dan Rivers told him that there is an American anecdote about a scrap car dealer who got himself a mixed wolf /dog thinking it would aggressively defend his lot from thieves. But the wolf dog, who was loyal and affectionate to his master, would mostly keep himself hidden away ! When strangers would arrive at the lot, he would hide himself, silently listening, watching and smelling, but almost never showing aggression unless it was feeding time and a human, other than its master, came between the wolf-dog and his food.

"That's fascinating !" comments Anna. "So if someone was keeping a wolf illegally and then released it when it grew too big it wouldn't necessarily mean that it would attack humans who presented no apparent threat." Anna crosses her fingers. She doesn't like the idea of an 'innocent' wolf being shot."

Roger adds, "there are cases of wild animals being kept and then dumped when they become too much to handle."

"M'mm", says Fernbank, "I'm not sure what to think. However, I have since heard from the Doc. He says that the victim was mostly likely to have been attacked by an animal, but rather than a wolf, it would seem maybe more likely to have been a large dog attack. After the attack, possibly dead or dying, he appears to have been finally slashed to pieces. perhaps with some kind of serrated knife, or a razor to make it look like part of the animal attack. The idea of a large dog came to mind, although it's unlikely to have struck at random. Of course, if a person had trained such a dog to attack perceived 'prey' this may have been the idea, for the murderer to fool us into thinking that Tom Preston had been the victim of a wild animal attack rather than murdered."

"So, are we looking for a human attacker ?" asks PC Jones.

"Could it be a man wearing a fur coat ?" grins PC Walker.

There's muted laughter.

Fernbank silences the team with a severe look. "Listen, the style of the attack could have been a ruse to put us off the scent ! I'm not ruling out an animal attack, but maybe with the presence of its owner. As DS Kinsale has pointed out there could be wild animals kept illegally and released when they become too large to handle, but that is only one suggestion. At the moment, we keep our eyes and ears open. "

A few more sniggers, halted by a dirty look from DCI Fernbank.

Finally, jobs are allocated and informers and 'grasses' (informants) are to be spoken to in order to see if the names of any likely candidates arise.

"Check all the grapevines," instructs the DCI. "Right then. Clear off !"

(4) A New Investigation

"You can't go back and change the beginning, but you can start where you are and change the ending." (CS Lewis)

Anna Kinsale had originally shared a flat with an old school friend, Laura. It was in a convenient location, situated near Woodstone in Essex, on the outskirts of London. Laura had got married back in April and Anna had needed to find a new flat-mate to share the costs as she wanted to stay put.

The flat occupies the top floor of a three storey terraced red-brick house, dating back to Edwardian times. There is a bedroom for each tenant. Also, shared, is a small bathroom and an open-plan living/dining/kitchen area.

Anna and Laura had originally decorated each room themselves. The rooms had been dull and gloomy. Anna had made Laura laugh by describing it as being like a scene from a black and white horror movie. On first seeing the flat, the grimy, cracked glass of the windows cast an eerie glow into the dusty room. Thick cobwebs hung on every surface. The women's footsteps had echoed, sounding deafening on the cold, wooden floors. When Anna had asked if they could make changes, the grumpy landlord, who looked as unloved as the flat, had muttered "do what you like." So, Anna and Laura had made the place their own. Now the rooms were all decorated in a clean and fresh white, the fashion of the day. The living room had a large silvery grey, silky rug. Two modern armchairs were each covered with a brilliant green throw, complemented by orange cushions. A small, orange circular bistro table and chairs completed the furnishings. Modern pieces of abstract art exploded their rainbow colours across the room.

On a fine day, the living room was bathed in light and overlooked an attractive, open area known as 'The Flats'. This open land constituted the southern-most portion of Epping Forest. The location suited Anna perfectly. The open area gave her security. She had been brought up in a village just over the Essex border. She had spent her youth in the countryside. She had always felt that the trees afforded her a feeling of safety that the concrete and glass of the capital did not. This location was a link with home. On the other hand, it was close to her workplace and convenient for the West End with its shopping and eating outlets.

Anna had advertised for a new flatmate in the Evening Post. About a month earlier, she'd had an enquiry from a woman named Philomena O'Farrell. Anna had invited her over to see the flat and have a chat. Philomena was a striking looking woman of about Anna's own age – late twenties. She had red hair, green eyes and a soft, lilting Irish accent. Anna immediately felt a bond with Philomena. She discovered her potential flatmate was a nurse at the London Hospital at Whitechapel, only a short ride away on the Tube. The pair liked one another right away. Anna took Philomena for a drink at the local tavern known as 'The Dick Turpin', named after the infamous highwayman who is said to have been buried in Epping Forest. By the end of the evening, they were flatmates. Philomena was to move in the following week.

Anna later learned that Philomena was a Catholic. She had hung a little crucifix on the wall of her bedroom as well as placing a small statue of Mary, Mother of Jesus, on her chest of drawers. She didn't attend Mass on Sundays though. Anna never liked to ask about this.

Occasionally, Philomena would ask Anna about cases she was working on. Anna only gave her the information that could be found in the public arena, newspapers and so on. One evening, when she returned home, Philomena had been in the flat for most of the day. She'd just finished a turn of night shifts. Having slept during the morning, she had busied herself with shopping and tidying the flat. She'd bought ingredients for their supper and had planned an omelette with a side salad for them both, followed by strawberry ice cream.

When they sat down to eat their supper, Philomena asked Anna about the death of a young man whose body had been discovered in Epping Forest. Apparently, the local newspapers were speculating about an attack by a pack of savage wolves or even werewolves !

Anna reveals that it was believed by the police that this may have been a mistake and the young man had died from extensive stab wounds. She knew this would be reported in the next day's papers, but it was clear that locals were not going to change their minds in a hurry. A wolf attack was far more interesting !

After supper, once they had cleared away the dishes, the pair sit down in the living area. Anna senses that Philomena is not going to let the matter drop. Philomena's keen to know as much as possible about the wolf theory. Gradually, as they chat, Anna discovers that Philomena is fascinated by wolves and their significant role in Irish mythology and history, with its symbolism and associations evolving over long periods of time to reflect the changing beliefs and values of Irish society.

Anna had also noticed that Philomena always wore a little gold crucifix on a chain around her neck. Also on the chain was a little wolf's head carved in silver. She asks Philomena about this.

Philomena explains, "the meaning or symbolism of the Wolf is reflected in the wearing of wolf pendants. The three most important qualities the wolf's head represents are strength, resilience and power. Wearing a pendant like mine as a talisman is believed to give the person wearing it a sense of inner strength and courage."

"It's beautiful," says Anna, studying it closely.

"You see," continues Philomena, "wolves are social animals that live in packs, and they are known for their fierce loyalty to their family members. A wolf pendant like this represents the importance of family and the bond between us and our loved ones. It also is a symbol of a close connection to the spiritual realm. In Irish Celtic cultures, wolves are seen as spiritual guides who can help individuals tap into their intuition and inner wisdom."

"Wow"!

"I wear both the cross and the wolf's head to show the important link between Christianity and Ancient Celtic beliefs. From a woman's point of view, I like the idea that wolves are also associated with freedom and independence.

Wolf pendants are also a reminder of the importance of individuality and self-reliance."

Anna also learns that in a spiritual world, creatures, such as wolves, are far older than Humankind. They have a closer relationship with the natural world because they are such an integral part of it.

Philomena adds, "We ignore the call of the wild at our own peril. The human race has lost that connection. Those lucky people who seek it and find it, gain extra senses that humans have, in the main, lost."

The pair sit quietly, taking in all that has been discussed.

Philomena adds, "Once upon a time, the wolf ranged right across the Northern Hemisphere in all kinds of terrain. In fact, the wolf was so widespread in Ireland that the country was once nicknamed "Wolf Land" !"

The two women are drinking white wine. They toast one another and the wolves.

Later, as she lies in bed, Anna mulls over their conversation. In this modern capitalist and materialistic world, she thinks, it's true that people have distanced themselves from a sympathetic and empathetic view of such animals. She has always felt uncomfortable about zoos and keeping animals imprisoned rather than running free. Philomena had said that such animals' spiritual and empathetic bonds with humans have been broken over time.

Anna also considers what Philomena has said about issues such as climate change and what's called 'global warming'. Philomena explained that she had joined a group called

'Friends of the Earth' which is now just being formed. Apparently, they want to make people's rejection of care for our natural world more public. Philomena gave Anna the example of where, in the wild, animals interfere with modern humans and our control of the planet. They are perceived as a threat. They are considered less important than people. This is a mistake for the worth of the animal should not be measured by us and our selfish desires. Anna is fascinated by such ideas. She falls asleep with all this information buzzing in her head.

(5) On the Trail of the Epping Forest Murderer

"There is always an adventure waiting in the woods."

(Katelyn S. Bolds)

Anna has been thinking hard about the murder of Tom Preston. Such a terrible way to die, made worse by the thought of it being someone so young. The investigating team are now considering the murder as possibly being connected to drugs and drug trafficking. There have been a number of cases of drugs being sold and used by young people and even the homeless in the area. The latter are coerced into drug dealing as they are seen as people who don't want to come in contact with the law and can easily be forced to do as they are told. Many become drug addicts themselves. They then need a fix to be provided, which in turn depends on them working for the drug dealers.

Anna wonders to herself what does it take for such an apparently decent young man to get involved ? Who coerced him ? She knows it won't be easy to find someone who is willing to shine a light on the darkest of people and places and help to take the real action required to stop it. Was Tom a vulnerable person ? How was he intimidated into such a dreadful world ? Anna guesses the task for the investigating team is to find a way of shining light and let the voices of the victims of such a heinous crime be heard.

Anna has come to the conclusion, over her time in the police force, that beyond survival and necessary comfort for good health of body and mind, criminal acts, especially involving drug cartels, need to be shown up as the greed that reaches out and damages members of society, often the young. It also damages whole communites.

She arrives at the nick early this morning. It's very warm already and looks like becoming a blazing hot day. Sunlight streams golden shafts through the office window in an announcement of the risen sun.

Anna, as a detective, feels lucky to be in plain clothes, wearing a skirt and blouse, rather than the heavy serge uniforms that WPCs wear. Many of the women would like to wear trousers, which they think to be far more suitable and practical than skirts, especially when pursuing criminals on foot ! Rumour has it that the Queen's dressmaker, Norman Hartnell, has been asked to design a new style of uniform for London's Metropolitan WPCs. Anna is doubtful though that this will include trousers.

It's only 8am, but when she reaches their shared office, Roger is already there. He proudly presents her with a cup of tea.

"Went for one myself so thought you'd be here bright and early too."

"Thanks." Things are looking up in terms of the relationship with her partner.

Anna tells Roger about her conversation with her flat-mate around the subject of wolves.

"Interesting, but I think Frank's going to follow the idea of drugs being involved. There's talk of Tom Preston arranging a picnic with his girlfriend so as to meet with a dealer. The wolf attack is still a possibility, but bearing in mind no wolves have been reported missing, going down that particular path now seems less likely."

"M'mm, " says Anna, "but the Doc suggested a wild animal attack or even a big dog. If he was meeting a dealer, maybe he had a big, viscious dog. That would explain the injuries."

As they finish their tea, Frank Fernbank arrives in the office."Morning both."

Anna and Roger greet the boss.

"The Doc left a message on my phone late last night. It seems that his initial findings are correct. There are signs of an animal attack, but more likely a dog. So, I reckon we're looking for a drug deaer with a nasty dog. It could even have been planned like a contract killing."

Anna asks. "Do we have any contenders ?"

Frank replies. "There must be some connection with the underworld. I think we should prioitise finding out more about Tom Preston."

"I checked," says Anna. "He doesn't have a criminal record. Of course, that doesn't mean he hasn't been involved in crime. He just hasn't been caught."

"M'mm," agrees Frank. "OK, both of you start asking round. Go back and ask the families again. Check place of work, neighbours, his contacts and his friends. "

Anna and Roger make their way to the car park and an unmarked police vehicle, a Hillman Avenger. Roger offers to drive. "I think we'll stick together." suggests Roger. Two detectives make the serious nature of the crime more obvious. I'll be the hard man and let you be all sympathy and understanding. Good combination, eh ?"

Anna nods. Interesting how men want to take the hard line and the women are expected to be kind and comforting. One day.......

They make a start with Tom's parents. A sorry looking Fred Preston answers the door. The two detectives are polite, making a sympathetic approach.

Roger begins. "We're sorry to intrude, Mr Preston, but we do want to catch Tom's killer and we would like to ask you some more questions."

"If you don't mind," adds Anna.

Mr Preston moves to one side and ushers them in.

He takes them into the living room. He leaves for a moment, calling his wife from the kitchen. Mrs Preston enters the room. Her eyes are still red from crying and she stoops miserably as she comes in. Mr Preston directs her to an armchair.

"These detectives want to ask us some questions, dear. They want to find the person who did this to Tom...." As he finishes speaking, his voice breaks. He sits down on another armchair and directs Anna and Roger to the sofa.

Mrs Preston asks if they would like a cup of tea.

"That's very kind of you," replies Anna, smiling sympathetically at this poor woman who has lost her only child.

Roger gives Anna a knowing look. "DS Kinsale will help you, won't you, Detective Sergeant ?"

Anna nods. The two women retreat to the kitchen. Anna puts water in the kettle and places it on the stove, whilst Mrs Preston busies herself with arranging cups and saucers on a tray.

"Call me Anna," by the way, says Anna kindly. It's Elsie isn't it ?"

Mrs Preston forces a smile. "Yes, dear."

"It's such a shame," says Anna.

"Elsie hesitates, then tells Anna. "Tom had proposed to his young lady. They're engaged you know. Poor Mary. " She hesitates and tries to hold back her tears. "We might have had grandchildren, you know." She looks at Anna with a forced smile.

Anna touches her arm in sympathy. "I promise you, Elsie, we'll make every effort to find the culprit." Anna brings the teapot over to the kettle. She takes a tin of tea leaves from a shelf, puts several spoonfuls in the teapot and then fills it with hot water from the kettle."

While the tea is brewing, Anna sits on a chair at the kitchen table and indicates to Elsie Preston to sit with her. "Can you think of anyone who might want to harm Tom ?

"Not really. He was a quiet, gentle lad. Not been in trouble with the police or anything like that. He loves....loved.... his job.

"He worked at Houghton's garage, didn't he ?"

"Yes. Reg Houghton is a friend of ours. Tom loves cars.....She breathes deeply.....loved. I can't get used to him not being here. I keep thinking he'll come home and everything will be normal. Tears roll down Mrs Preston's cheeks.

As Anna pours the tea into the cups and adds milk, Elsie reaches for her handkerchief and wipes away the tears. Anna picks up the tray and walks towards the door. Elsie follows.

Everyone drinks their tea. There is a tense silence for a few moments.

" I don't want revenge, says Mrs Preston suddenly. I'm a Catholic.There was a suggestion that a wolf might have attacked him."

"That's only one theory," explains Roger." We've found no evidence of wolves missing from zoos. No, I'm afraid, at present, it looks like an attack by a person." He didn't mention a dog. It seemed just too awful.

"If that is the case," says Mr Preston, "then as my wife says, we don't want revenge."

"Roger nods his head, but adds, " however, you do understand that if he is found and convicted, he will go to prison for a very long time. He looks at each of them.

For a moment there is silence. Then Mrs Preston speaks. "I'm from an Irish family you know. We believe that wolves are connected with emotions and feelings. Wolves care for children and young people, not kill them. I don't believe he was attacked by a wolf."

Roger and Anna exchange glances. This is a difficult one ! For a moment there is an uneasy silence.

Then Mrs Preston speaks. She has folded up her handkerchief full of tears, in her fist. "You see," she explains, making eye contact with both Anna and Roger. " 'sad' is an emotion of your inner good wolf. Your angel self if you're a Catholic like me. You must ask the good wolf for solutions. The desire for revenge must be cast off in favour of supportive love for those affected. Love and happy memories of those who have passed on to the Otherworld must outweigh hatred and anger, even when the death has been untimely and violent. When the time is right you will be reunited with your loved ones who have passed on.It's what Our Lord Jesus says as well."

There is a silence whilst they all finish their tea and consider Mrs Preston's words. When the tea cups and saucers have been returned to the tray, Roger turns to Mr Preston. "Is there anything you'd like to add, Mr Preston ?"

Fred Preston seems as if he's miles away. "Oh, er, no, I don't think so. My wife has said all there is to say."

Roger makes a move. Anna also stands up.

"Thank you both very much for your help at this difficult time," says Roger.

Anna presses Elsie's hand in sympathy. Mrs Preston's words have made her think.

"We promise to do everything we can to catch this person. We will need to speak with you again. Please ring us if you think of anything, however small, which might give us a clue for the attack on your son." Roger adds.

They both smile at the bereaved couple and make their way back to the car.

Roger takes the wheel. "So, anything interesting about the lad ?" he asks.

"Not really. Elsie said he was quiet and gentle. Not the sort of young man to get mixed up in anything dodgy."

"Maybe he witnessed something that he shouldn't have," suggests Roger.

"What about you ?" asks Anna.

"Mr Preston seemed a bit distant. Not surprising of course. He mentioned that his son worked at Houghton's Garage.

Owned by a chap called Reg Houghton. Let's give him a visit."

Houghton's Garage turned out to be a rather scruffy premises on the outskirts of Woodstone. As the pair enter the yard, there are several cars with their prices indicated on their windscreens. Anna might have described them as 'old wrecks', or 'bangers'. The sound of an engine ticking over, accompanied by a clank of tools comes from the interior of the garage behind these vehicles. The pair step into the garage. There is a movement and a middle-aged man, his face grimy with grease, emerges from an inspection pit, wiping his hands with a dirty cloth as he does so.

"Can I help you?" he asks coldly, looking them both over as he speaks.

Roger speaks first. "I'm Detective Inspector Edwards and this…" He indicates Anna. "…is Detective Sergeant Kinsale. We're from Woodstone Police Station."

The man, who they assume is Reg Houghton himself, speaks. He looks at them with a wary eye. "I presume you're here to ask about Tom Preston ?"

"That's right," confirms Roger.

"I don't know what to say," says Reg stonily. He doesn't speak, but rubs dirt from his face with his age-spotted hand. "Bit of a shock. Nice young fella. What happened ? There's all this nonsense in the papers about him being attacked by a wolf."

"That doesn't appear to be the case," explains Roger, anxious to quash the wolf theory. "I can't tell you any more at this stage in the investigation, but a full investigation is underway."

"I understand," says Reg, looking uncomfortable and saying no more.

Anna speaks. "Mr Houghton, we're trying to find out if Tom had any enemies. Someone who held a grudge maybe."

Reg Houghton shrugs his shoulders. "I can't think of anyone offhand. Tom got on well with me and Tony."

"Tony?" queries Roger.

"Tony's a mechanic here. Fully qualified. Nice bloke. Good worker. I can't believe he'd be involved in anything like that."

Does anyone else work here ?" asks Anna.

"Only my wife, Sheila. She answers the phone, sees to the paperwork...sending out invoices, etc."

"Is Sheila here ?" asks Anna.

"Yeah. Hang on, I'll give her a call." Reg walks across to a room at the side of the garage. "You there, love ?"

A tubby, grey-haired woman in her fifties appears from what is presumably the office.

"This is my wife," says Reg. "Maureen Houghton."

"Roger holds out his hand. "Nice to meet you, Mrs Houghton. I'm Detective Inspector Edwards." He points to Anna. "My colleague, Detective Sergeant Kinsale."

"You're here about Tom," I suppose. "All that rubbish about a wolf attack. The papers should be ashamed of themselves."

"Clearly, we don't believe now that is the case," says Roger firmly, confirming his previous comment to Mr Houghton..

Anna chips in. "We're looking for any possible enemies of Tom. Maybe someone he argued with ?"

Maureen looks at her husband. Then back at Anna. "We've racked our brains. There isn't anyone we can think of. Tom was such a gentle, polite lad. I can't think how he could have annoyed someone enough for them to murder him."

"OK, well thanks for your help. We may need to speak with you again."

Roger asks, "where can we find Tony, the mechanic. What's his surname ?

"Blake. It's his day off" explains Mr Houghton."He usually goes fishing……he'll be back here tomorrow morning."

"Thanks, we'll call back."

Anna and Roger bid the couple farewell.

"Bit of a dead end," grumbles Roger. "We'll have to look further afield."

---

(6) Taking a Break

"Disconnect to reconnect." (anon)

Anna is just leaving the police station. She's meeting Murray later at their favourite pub, The Blue Boar. It's situated only a short walk from her flat. It gives her time to get home, draw breath and take a relaxing bath.

Being on a date with Murray, for Anna, is always a great way to relax. They are good company for one another. The chemistry is there, but they are able to be the best of friends too. Both being in the police force, means that they can discuss cases if necessary and know that they have spoken in confidence. That said, they try to restrict such discussions when they are on a date because they want to be able to relax and enjoy one another's company without the subject of crime rearing its ugly head !

When Anna arrives home around 6pm, her flatmate, Philomena is relaxing on the sofa with a book. She jumps up, greets Anna and offers to make her a cuppa. Anna nods gratefully.

Anna sits on an armchair and tries to relax by closing her eyes and steadying her breathing. Whenever she is stressed she likes to go somewhere quiet and sit still for a time, letting the feelings and ideas wash over her like the tide brushing the shore. Then, when she's ready, she counts her blessings one by one. It helps to turn her around. Make her feel more positive. After that, she rests some more, until she's ready to reface her challenges. Anna opens her eyes as Philomena sets the tea tray down on a small table. While Philomena pours out the tea, Anna helps herself to one of the chocolate biscuits which accompany the tea. By the time she has eaten the biscuit and leaned across to pick up her teacup, she is already feeling calmer.

"Busy day ?" asks Philomena.

"Bit of a nasty one. Can't say much yet."

Philomena is aware that Anna can't give out too many details in serious cases. Usually, the newspapers report what they can glean, although not always truthfully. Making eye-popping headlines can involve a journalist's vivid imagination. Philomena knows better than to ask too many questions.

Anna knows Philomena is on night duty at the hospital. That usually means a 10pm start.

"Thought I'd make an omlette. Do you fancy one ? asks Philomena.

"No thanks. I'm having a quick wash and brush up and then off to meet Murrray at the pub…. I expect you'll be gone by the time I get back."

Philomena winks at her. "Don't worry, the coast will be clear if you want to bring a visitor home."

Both women laugh.

After drinking their tea, Philomena heads to the kitchen to prepare her supper. Anna heads for the bathroom.

As she lies in the warm water with the soft smell of the bathsalts in her nostrils, Anna relaxes. She puts the day's events to the back of her mind. She closes her eyes and thinks about her date. A date, naturally, has a physical time and place, yet the joy of it was to allow the lovers time to stand still in those beautiful moments, to the exclusion of anything else.

By the time she's ready to leave, Philomena has finished her meal and has returned to the sofa with her current reading choice. Anna bids her goodnight and sets off.

Anna has brought a shawl, which she thought she might need later, but the weather is still warm and the sky light. When she arrives at the pub, she finds Murray waiting for her outside. He takes her hand and stands back to admire her pretty summer dress.

"You look lovely, my dear," Murray tells her, winking as he speaks.

"Thank you kind sir," responds Anna. She gives a little swirl to show off her dress.

They make their way into the saloon bar. The bar is full. Conversations, exchanged in loud voices, fill the air. It's a live band night. Voices compete with the rock music that dominates the atmosphere. The crowd is mainly young. Murray winds his way through the warm bodies to order their drinks a pint of bitter and a shandy for Anna. Before the drink is poured he feels someone melting their body into his from behind. Anna has joined him.

"Want to sit outside ?" asks Murray.

Anna nods. Let's hear some music first !"

The band is called 'The Blues Boys' and they sound good. They're playing several well known numbers. The lead singer, known as Des, has a great voice. Anna and Murray don't speak for a while, just enjoying the music. After a time, the band stop for a break. Murray goes back to the bar to order more drinks. Anna moves to a bench outside, taking in her surroundings and relaxing into them.

Murray soon returns with more drinks. They deliberately avoid conversations about work. They discuss the music and enjoy just holding hands and appreciating the time and place. Finally, the band finish playing and shortly afterwards time is called by the landlord.

As Anna and Murray set off in the direction of Anna's flat, they watch the emerging starlight and the silvery moon. The shadows of the trees dance upon the fences surrounding the houses which line the route. They dapple the The Flats, the leaves flickering like candlelight, creating a new picture from moment to moment. Amid the perfume of the summer blooms, feeling the cool of the evening wash over them, Anna and Murray savour this moment together. From neighbouring gardens comes the music of laughter, the promise of playfulness and new joys to brighten their dreams.

---

(7) A Lupine Tale

"It may be reasonable to expect most people to dismiss the notion of a nurturing wolf as a naive person's referent, but that doesn't seem wise to me. When, from the prisons of our cities, we look out to wilderness, when we reach intellectually for such abstractions as the privilege of leading a life free from nonsensical conventions, or one without guilt or subterfuge—in short, a life of integrity—I think we can turn to wolves. We do sense in them courage, stamina, and a straightforwardness of living;

we do sense that they are somehow correct in the universe and we are somehow still at odds with it. As our sense of sharing the planet with other creatures grows—and perhaps that is ultimately the goal of natural history—the deep contemplation of wolves may be seen as part of an attempt to nurture the humbler belief that there is more to the world than mankind. In that sense, the wolf-mother is just now upon us, in a role a quantum leap removed from Romulus and Remus."

(Barry H Lopez in his book 'Of Wolves and Men'.)

When Anna and Roger arrive at the station the following day, there seems to be an air of general excitement. Voices gabbling nineteen to the dozen.

Anna catches the eye of the desk sergeant. "What's going on ?"

Sergeant Dennis explains. "The Met have been in touch. According to them, "one of their beat bobbies has had sight of a wolf. They're working with a vet from London Zoo to see if it can be found and tranquilised...or even shot, if they can't sedate it. They came to us because....well....the sighting was near Queen Elizabeth's Hunting Lodge. Our territory, Epping Forest.

A grinning PC White, adds. They told us the vet says, "do not approach the wolf if you see it."

There's general laughter.

The appearance of DCI Fernbank causes a sharp stop to the fun.

"Right. Listen up you lot. We are not taking this as a joke. Heads of local schools have been told not to let the pupils go outside. Plods will be in the area warning people. There's a van with a speaker going round. It's going to be on local radio and on television as well. However unlikely this seems, it could have very nasty consequences. It could be that there is a pair of wolves. If, while you're out, you get any...and I mean any, sight of, or information about, a wolf, you radio in. The animal expert from London University and their vet are to be informed about any sighting.

"How did the wolves escape ?" asks Anna.

Fernbank responds. "It seems the two wolves were in a private, unlicenced zoo and they escaped from their enclosure. They broke through a steel wire fence despite it being checked daily, the zoo owner has emphasised."

"Was it vandalism ?" asks Roger.

"Now that's where we get involved. Roger, I want you and Anna to go and interview this prat with the private zoo. Bring him here. He's committed an offence and will be prosecuted as he doesn't have a licence. We want him here to get as much info as possible on the likely results of this escape. Put the frighteners on him if he doesn't seem to accept the consequences of his actions. We need to know if it was an act of deliberate vandalism or inadequate fencing."

"Is this connected to the case of Tom Preston though ? The doc said he'd been murdered by a person, not a wolf ?" Roger asks.

"Just see what you can unearth," instructs Fernbank.

"No rest for the wicked," says Roger as he and Anna make their way to the car.

Following instructions, they make their way to the home of the wolves' owner, Peregrine Buckfast. The property turns out to be a large mansion set in acres of land on the far side of The Flats where the border of Epping Forest begins. Anna rings the doorbell. There's a pause and a man dressed as a butler appears."

We're from the police," explains Roger. "Our visit concerns the escaped wolves."

Both detectives hold up their ID cards.

The butler remains stony-faced. "This way please."

He heads them to a library. The old library has a few tall walls full of ancient volumes. Anna guesses most are now a sort of decoration to set the scene. They look dusty and unloved. A well dressed man wearing a dark-coloured suit, a colourful deep red cravat and matching pocket handkerchief, had been sitting at an antique oak desk. He stands up and turns to face them as the two detectives enter.

"How can I help you ?" the man enquiries politely.

"Police. I think you know why we're here," says Roger sharply, in an annoyed tone.

"Ah," is the man's response. "Well now, I'm struggling to comprehend how the wolves broke through the fence. They're quite tame. Used to people. I've had them since they were cubs."

"That maybe," continues Roger, "however, now that they are out of their enclosure and have made their way to a built-up area, neither you nor us can predict what might happen." He adds, "we, the police that is, are now investigating how the wolves escaped. You say there doesn't appear to be any deliberate damage to their enclosure. We can only deduce from this that the barrier was not adequate."

Anna chips in with, "we understand that the wolves escaped at 8 o'clock yesterday morning but you didn't contact us until today."

Peregrine Buckfast looked embarrassed. "You have to understand the area is continuously monitored by myself and my animal keeper. We have been trying to find how they escaped and where they might be.."

"Do you have a licence for housing these animals ?" Roger asks in a sharp tone.

Buckfast looks unhappy and wary....."well no. You see, they are pets."

"Wild animals are not pets, sir," says Roger in a gruff manner. "You may be prosecuted."

Buckfast looks at the floor as if studying something of interest on the parquet.

Anna tells him, "if we can get them tranquilised by a trained marksman working with a vet, we will do that. Sadly, the alternative will be to have them shot."

"No, no," gasps Buckfast. "You can't do that ! They wouldn't hurt anyone.'

"We can't take that risk though, Mr Buckfast." Roger now speaks in an authoritative voice. "You don't have a licence for keeping wolves. A wolf is classified as a dangerous wild animal. That is why lethal force may be appropriate now that the animals have breached the perimeter of your land."

Buckfast looks as if he is close to tears. "Please don't harm them. They are not dangerous," he emphasises.

"I'm afraid you will have to accompany us to the police station Mr Buckfast." states Roger firmly.

Anna assures him that an animal specialist from London University and a vet will follow the wolves' whereabouts and advise on any action to be taken. "Shooting them would only be a last resort, " she emphasises. Privately, she is less sure about this, but she's trying to placate Peregrine Buckfast. She feels sorry because he clearly loves the creatures. She thinks of the nature of wolves as explained to her by the animal expert and Philomena. She feels sad.

---

(8) Wolves on the Loose

"What great big eyes you have, Grandma." said Little Red Riding Hood.
"All the better to see you with," the Wolf replied.

Back at home, Anna has just had a bath and is thinking about putting her feet up with a good book. She keeps thinking about the childhood story of Red Riding Hood and how she loved being scared when her dad, reading it to her, used his 'scary wolf voice' !

As she emerges from the bathroom, she hears the front door opening and a cheery voice calling "anybody home ?" It's Philomena.

"Hang on," calls Anna. She goes to the bedroom and slips on her dressing gown, having wrapped her wet hair in a towel. She crosses the landing into the living room.

"Busy day ?" asks Philomena.

Anna knows she's keen to hear about progress in the case of the missing wolves. She doesn't mention to Philomena that the police case has been nicknamed 'Grandma', from the story of Red Riding Hood. "Not much news really. There are two wolves that escaped and we've got a marksman with a tranquiliser gun and a vet standing by." Anna doesn't mention the last resort of shooting the animals.

As if Anna's thoughts have permeated her brain, Philomena says, "I do hope you find them and they are unharmed. They won't kill them will they ?"

Anna looks awkwardly at the floor and doesn't speak.

"You mean they might shoot them if they can't be caught ?"

Anna keeps her head down and mutters; "we hope it won't come to that. We've been given an explanation by an expert that an escaped wolf is unlikely to attack humans, unless they interfere with it or threaten it."

"Oh......"

There follows an awkward silence. Finally, Philomena says, "how about a G & T ?"

Anna nods sadly.....

Moments later, Philomena hands the drink she has mixed to Anna. She smiles. "It's not your fault, Anna. I understand it's out of your hands."

"Thanks," is the reply. Anna hesitates. She knows the situation is going to continue for a while. She decides to ask Philomena to tell her more about the Irish wolves. She might even learn something which could help to save the pair of escapees.

Philomena stays still and calm, as if getting herself in the mood for story-telling. "Well now," she begins, "the Celts believed, many still do, that the wolf is a powerful symbol of the moon. Believers think that the creature is connected to transformation, intuition, and the hunt. They also believe that wolves have the ability to communicate with the spirits of the dead, and that they are therefore able to act as intermediaries between the living and the dead. If you take the case you're dealing with, it's my belief that our forefathers understood the wolf much better than we do in more recent times. The ancient Celts, as well as other groups, for example, the Native Americans, felt that they are an integral part of the natural world. However, with the arrival of Christianity in Ireland, the wolf began to be seen as a symbol of evil and darkness. The Bible refers to wolves as predators and destroyers and this negative view of the animal began to permeate Irish and other American and European societies. By the Middle Ages, the wolf had become a symbol of fear and terror, and many people believed that they were agents of the devil. As a result of this fear, the wolf was hunted to extinction in Ireland. By the 17th century, the last wolf was believed to have been killed, and the animal disappeared. Only to exist in Irish folklore and mythology."

Anna is enthralled.

Philomena continues. "Wolves were the last of Britain's top predators to be hunted to extinction. It's believed they disappeared sometime in the 18th century in England, following centuries of persecution."

Philomena finishes by telling Anna that in very recent years there has been a resurgence of interest in the wolf. "There is a growing group of people who are now beginning to work towards reintroducing the wolf to Ireland's wildest landscapes. So you see, not so far into the future, if Britain followed suit, your missing pair could indeed be free to roam the forests and wild areas."

"Just like Epping Forest," laughs Anna.

Philomena pours them another drink. They then decide to take a walk and on the way home, enjoy fish and chips. The Flats, the open area close to their home, is part of the original forest, now having only a few trees, but used by people as a natural public park. As they walk along, eating their fare from the newspaper wrapping, Philomena looks round and says "wouldn't it be wonderful if we saw the pair here ?"

Anna smiles nervously.

---

(9) Where is Tony Blake ?

"Me would like an invisibility cloak to get the hell out of this mess."

(Jandy Nelson, The Sky Is Everywhere)

Anna and Roger arrive at Woostone nick early. They had returned to the garage where Tom Preston worked several times to meet the other mechanic, Tony Blake. However, several days have passed and there's been no sign of him. The garage owner, Reg Houghton appears puzzled. According to him, Tony hadn't asked for any time off and neither had he phoned in sick. Reg tells the two officers that Tony had always seemed such a reliable chap.

"It's a mystery to me," Reg adds.

"What do you know about Tony's private life ?" asks Roger.

"Not a lot," is the response. "I don't press people to talk if they don't want to. No, he was a quiet one. Got on with his work. No bother." Reg shrugs his shoulders.

"Do you know anything about his family ? Friends ?" asks Anna.

"No, as I say, he was never very forthcoming."

Anna persists. "How did he get on with Tom Preston ? Were they friends ?"

"I wouldn't have said so. Tony's older than Tom. Apart from the car trade, I don't think they had much in common."

Reg turns to return to the garage where he is repairing a car.

"OK. Thanks," calls Anna to Reg's disappearing back.

Anna and Roger look at one another.

"We have got his address," says Roger. "Let's pay him a visit."

The two detectives return to the car. They drive to the address they have been given. It's in a run-down area. A group of children are playing football in the street. Roger edges the car forward and the children stand in front of it, daring the driver to run them over.

"Police" shouts Roger from the wound-down car window.

"Coppers' shrieks a voice. The motley crew take to their heels and disappear around the corner out of sight.

The two police officers leave the car and walk towards the given address. The brightly painted front door is half off its hinges. The half-removed metal door knocker dangles, helped by gravity. The path is broken brickwork. They make their way to the entrance carefully avoiding pieces of brick sticking up from the ground. The mortar on the front wall of the house is holding back the weeds, but it too is crumbling.

"Looks like a bad sign," says Anna.

Roger nods. They enter. "Anyone home ?" calls Roger and his voice echoes through the dilapidated premises.

It's clear that If there had been anyone here they'd have heard him and either come out fighting or, more likely, fled already.

"Bugger", complains Roger.

They make their way through almost bare rooms. Just a few items of dirty, dust-covered furniture. From grubby windows to peeling paint, it certainly doesn't look as if anyone has been here very recently. There is dust collecting on all the surfaces, sparkling in the sunlight pouring through the broken living room window. The kitchen has dirty pots and pans on the draining board and in the sink, but the remains are hard and dry. Not very recent. Cobwebs decorate the ceiling. There is a bed in the larger of the bedrooms with a ffilthy mattress and a lone blanket. If Tony Blake has been camping here, it certainly looks as if he has been gone for a while. Just an address to give his employer perhaps.

"He's certainly gone. Probably done a runner," states Roger.

"Looks like it."

Anna spots a couple of dog ends in an over-flowing ashtray. She lifts them to her nose and smells them. "Cannabis," she says.

" Right. Well this could be just the tip of the iceberg. If Blake killed Tom, or one of a gang he belonged to did, it would explain the hasty retreat. The cannabis suggests that it's drug taking, could be drug dealing. Could even be on a big scale. This bloke, Tony Blake, may have just been a small cog, but in a very big machine. Otherwise, why the need to murder young Tom Preston ?"

Roger suggests Anna returns to the station and gets a forensic team there to go over the place with a fine tooth comb. "I'll stay here in case anyone returns. You take the car back to the station. We'll have to get an observation set up. Blake or others could return here.

Anna agrees. As she drives she thinks about the awful nature of the drug scene. Drug dealing, selling or supplying drugs of any type or quantity is becoming rife these days. People, like Tony Blake, may be small-time dealers who sell small quantities to offset the costs of their own drug use, or, more likely, in view of a murder being committed, there can be highly organised groups that operate like an organised crime business. She reminds herself there's no proof of any of this at this moment, but gut instinct tells her otherwise. It's one job for the police. Anna knows more training is necessary as drug use and dealing become more prolific. 'We have to be willing to shine a light on this trade which is polluting many young people's lives,' she says to herself.

---

(10) The Hunt is On.

"There's something stalking us. Off to the side of the road, moving through the forest.'

(Robin Hobb in 'Assassin's Fate')

Frustratingly for Anna, Roger is taking over the case of finding Tony Blake for now. In the meantime, there's another matter.

The wolf-hunting team is gathered and ready for action early this morning. DCI Fernbank begins. "We have invited these two specialists from the University of London." He indicates a tall, thin, middle-aged man as being Doctor (an academic title) James Knock. The man smiles at the gathering. Fernbank then points to a red-haired woman, perhaps in her mid thirties. "This is Professor Madeleine Jenkins who is also a qualified vet." Madeleine gives everyone a pleasant smile. The DCI pauses. He then states emphatically, "I want you to listen very carefully to these experts."

James Knock begins. "If you ever come across this pair of wolves, that we think will stick together – the pack instinct – remember that contrary to popular beliefs, propped up by childhood stories and films and books about wolves, they are thought of as fierce, man-eating carnivores. This is untrue. Wolves aren't hunters of humans. They don't want any interaction with humans, especially like herds of police officers with raised truncheons charging after them !"

There's general laughter.

"Seriously," continues James, "in the event of a confrontation, the most important advice is to stay calm and not use your voice ! Wolves are inquisitive and curious about humans they come in contact with. Stay still. They may have a sniff of the air when close to you, but it's most unlikely they'll get too close. Once they've satisfied themselves you aren't a threat, they'll leave. It's during or just after that time when the tranquiliser gun can be used."

Everyone is listening intently and making notes.

James continues. "Don't for the love of God, or wolf, try and intimidate them by howling....."

There's general laughter.

"Seriously though, you must remember that they are already edgy enough, one false move or sound and there's a chance, however small, that would be enough to get you overstepping their boundaries. They may be used to their owner and his employee, but strangers could mean a threat. At the end of the day, just remember they're just curious."

"Anything to add, Professor ?" asks Fernbank, turning to Madeline.

She explains, "As you know these two wolves are a rarity in Britain. Sadly, in most of Europe, wolves were driven to extinction centuries ago. I'm proud to say, I'm a conservationist. There's a small group of us who would love to reintroduce wolves to our wilder areas. If we can capture this pair, we could send them to a safe sanctuary which is being set up in East Anglia. As predators, wolves can actually make a vital contribution to a healthy ecosystem in areas where deer and other creatures have over-bred and are damaging wild areas. We are trying out today, baited foot hold traps. That sounds cruel, but we need to have them still so that a well-aimed tranquiliser dart will do the rest. I am desperately keen, as is James, to use these non-lethal methods."

"So," adds James. "Any questions ?

Silence.

DCI Fernbank takes over. "Right, you have each been given a partner to work with. Each pair has been given an advice sheet and a map of the area, with a grid marking the area each pair are to cover. There are also some groups like yours from The Met. If you do locate the wolves, you report in immediately, so that the team who are going to try and tranquilise the animals can get to you quickly. Keep your distance."

The atmosphere is tense. Everyone has the feeling they are on a quest.

DS Anna Kinsale is excited, but nervous about this special and important task. She is in charge of a group of three uniformed constables. PCs Lily Saunders, Tim Stretton and Joe Marshall.

She gathers them round her. "We have also been warned that capture techniques must be applied by experienced individuals only. If we locate them, we call in to HQ and keep an eye from a distance. Follow, but do not get too close. If you look at our area on the map, you'll see that we're starting from Forest View Road. You probably all know that this is the edge of the forest, where the trees begin. We stick together in pairs. Myself and Tim will go further up the road and cautiously make our way into the trees on the North side. Joe and Lily, you follow the trail to the South side. There will be two other teams heading East and West. 'You've got your walkie-talkies to keep in touch with HQ .....Tally Ho' " she grins.

As they set off, Anna remembers Philomena telling her that we know that man's best friend, the dog, evolved from wolves, most probably from friendlier wolves fed by kind humans centuries ago. Throughout the years of evolution, explained Philomena, wolves became closer to our ancestors and became their hunting companions. Their teeth grew smaller, muzzles became shorter, and overall size got shorter until they became the dogs we have today.

Anna and her companion, PC Tim Stretton, make their way cautiously into the outskirts of Epping Forest. Soon, the track they are following fades away. Anna remembers as a child, the family had picnics in the forest. She had felt the trees were hugging her. The branches were arms enfolding her in their canopy of shades of green. She had always felt the forest had a welcoming spirit to visitors such as herself and her family. It still felt as if there was something inside herself that the trees could feel. The breeze made the leaves wave a friendly greeting. Despite the question of wolves, she felt excited, yet calm at the same time.

After a short time, they find themselves in a clearing. Suddenly, sunlight returns. Here, there is a softness to the woodland floor and the moss softens and supports their feet and then springs back when the walkers have passed. The woodland is the birdsong. It is the playful light and the serenity of time that flows without the worry of clocks.

Anna's pleasurable thoughts are interrupted. Tim whispers to her "Did you hear something ?"

Anna stands still and strains to listen. Moments later she thinks she spies a shadowy shape ahead of them in the undergrowth. They both stand still.

Ahead of them is a small clearing enclosed by trees . They stop and listen intently. Beyond the clearing are more trees, edged by dense bramble. They follow a narrow gully that looks as if it has been cut as a path between the thorns. They follow it through a zigzag, turning into another enclosed clearing, All they can hear is the gentle rustling of the leaves. They are in a kind of twilight. Even the sun is hidden by the thickness of the trees. No sight or evidence of wild animals. Anna imagines the wolves moving through the forest on their travels, as if they were one with the trees and the dry summer earth. She remembers that when the police officers were being briefed on the behaviour of wolves and how to react to them, one expert quoted from a book he had read which included an account from a man called Alda Orton who was an Alaskan trapper :

"Howl It was wild, untamed music and it echoed from the hillsides and filled the valleys. It sent a queer shivering feeling along my spine. It was not a feeling of fear, you understand, but a sort of tingling, as if there was hair on my back and it was hackling."

The police teams had been told that the wolves could weigh around 6 or 7 stone and stand over 2 feet tall. The senses and emotions of wolves which prompt a howl remain unknown. Group howling has a quality of camaraderie about it they learned. This pair of wolves, it was believed, would attempt to remain together. Apparently, wolves greet each other with energetic tail wagging, just like dogs, and they each will have a general sense of good feeling when they are together. This might elicit howling which would inform the searchers that they are close to them. The wolf is tied by subtle invisible threads to the woods it moves through. The advice was not to get too close and report any sightings or possible sightings to the expert teams via a walkie-talkie so that they could then take over. Under no circumstances should they approach the wolves. Track and trace is the order of the day.

As the two officers proceed, suddenly, in the near distance, they hear what Anna is sure is a howl. They both listen intently. Yes, it has to be. No other nearby wildlife could match that sound.

The howl seems to remain at the same volume, suggesting one wolf, at least, has stopped travelling, The pair arrive at a place where the trees thin out and a large clearing emerges. On the far side of the clearing, on the edge of more trees, a wolf has settled. The overhanging trees have made the air a little cooler. It has lain down to rest on a patch of earth on the far side of a large rock. The police officers watch as the wolf's ears begin to flicker. Has he picked up their scent ? The animal must have been sleeping, but now begins to wake up.

Anna and Tim watch, entranced as the wolf rolls on his back and lies still with his front legs pointed upward. His back legs are splayed, His nose and tail curve towards each other as he relaxes. After a few minutes he flops over onto his side. The two police officers hold their breath as the wolf stands up, stretches, and moves a few feet away. Suddenly, the animal bounds forward, away from the watching pair. They watch as he gains speed.

Anna uses her walkie-talkie to contact HQ. She explains what they have seen and which direction the wolf has taken. As they edge ahead to try and follow its path, they hear the wolf howl. This time it's a long wail that quickly reaches a high pitch. Moments later, the wolf's partner appears. Anna assumes this is the female. She is smaller and trots delicately through the trees. The other wolf stands watching her approach. They greet each other and approach each other, tails erect. When they meet each other they make high squeaking noises and encircle each other, rubbing and pushing, poking their noses into each other's neck fur, backing away to stretch, chasing each other playfully for a few steps, They stand quietly together for a minute or two. Then the pair depart, moving quickly and quietly through the trees, away from the trail they had been on. Then, suddenly they are gone, the female in front. Having advised Detective Sergeant Jenkins of their location and the direction the wolves have taken, Anna and Tim move forward to watch as the wolves move away. They follow, keeping their distance.

As they approach a larger open area, they can see the wolves making their way into another part of the forest. Just as the animals reach the edge of the trees, Anna and Tim see three people walking stealthily towards them. Anna's heart is beating faster as the trio approach. They want to get as close as possible with the tranquiliser gun. They form a line and then approach in a 'U' shape. Anna notices with a shock that another of the animals' followers has a shotgun. She wants to close her eyes. She fears the result of the meeting of humans with wolves. As she watches, she becomes aware that the wolves have sensed the approach of the trio following as they edge closer. Suddenly, almost without warning, the man holding the tranquiliser gun takes aim and fires one shot, then another, seconds later. The wolves momentarily seem puzzled. Then they turn and press on, aiming for the cover of the trees.

Tim remarks that the expert had told them that the tranquilizer dart could take fifteen minutes to take effect. He and Anna recall being told that the drug which is administered causes changes in the brain similar to a human nap, but a much deeper sleep. Initially, the animals will be completely unaware. Within 15 minutes, they will be fully asleep.

A vehicle has parked close by. Once the wolves are asleep, they are both carefully placed aboard. Apparently, they will be taken to the registered Sanctuary in Suffolk where they can remain on a more permanent basis. There, they will have an area of pasture and woodland to investigate and make their own.

Once the wolves are under the influence of the dart, the crew help the wolves into a safe, comfortable position. Then load them carefully into the special vehicle, designed to accommodate larger animals. Once the work is done and the ride to the Sanctuary is completed, the veterinarians will give another drug to wake the wolves up. Anna and Tim watch, fascinated, from a distance and note how carefully the wolves are handled.

Soon afterwards, the vehicle leaves. Anna radios in and she and Tim make their way back to the police station. As they approach the outskirts of the City, they watch as in the hush of a deepening blue sky comes evening in the capital, ever lit up, ever awake, its heart ever pulsating.

---

(11) The Mysterious Murder of Tom Preston

"The unknown holds endless possibilities."(anon)

Anna has spent her lifetime growing up and now working on the outskirts of Epping Forest. The ancient woodland is well established as a habitat for a range of creatures, grassland, heath, streams, bogs and ponds, It straddles the border between Greater London and Essex. Most of the forest stretches from Epping in the north, down to The Flats on the periphery of London's built-up area. As it stretches towards the city, the forest narrows, and forms a kind of green corridor that extends deep into East London, as far as a place aptly named, Forest Gate. The Forest's unique position gave rise to its nickname, 'The Cockney Paradise'. Picnics and walks are popular in the daytime and at night it's popular with courting couples !

The extensive urban areas on the Forest's doorstep bring many visitors from outside the area to the Forest, and, sadly, they do cause a strain on the Forest's ecology. In the previous century local recreational users of the Forest had worked hard to preserve and take care of the Forest when it was threatened with enclosure and destruction in the late 19th century. The huge public outcry led the City of London Corporation to buy and save the site in what was the first major success of the budding environmental movement in Europe. Even now, in the mid-twentieth century, the Corporation still owns the Forest.

This so-called environmental milestone came at a cost. Early conservators didn't understand the human impact that shaped the forest and its ecosystems. They stopped pollarding trees and allowed animal grazing to decline. This changed the character of the Forest and led to reduced biodiversity. A renewed interest in the last few years by newly forming environmental groups is examining future care. Anna had learned from Philomena that she was a member of one such group. This pleased Anna because the forest had been her playground as a child and now a lovely place to wander and relax when away from her demanding job. Anna can't help feeling sorry that such a dreadful crime, the murder of Tom Preston, could have been committed in such a haven.

Anna looks at her watch. It reads 7.30 am. There's no noise, so she guesses that Philomena is still asleep. She wants to be at work by 8 o'clock. She hurriedly gets dressed and rushes downstairs. After a quick bowl of cereal she dashes out to her MG sports car and shoots off into the usual traffic jam as commuters arrrive in droves. Buses add to the slow speed and Anna taps her steering wheel in frustration. At a few minutes to 8, she arrives at Woodstone nick and parks her car in one of the few spaces at the back of the station.

Sometimes, if there are no spaces, she has to park in the nearby public car park.

As she heads to the station entrance, she notices that Frank Fernbank's grey Austin 1100 is already parked. She makes her way to the office where the DCI is busy sorting out some paperwork.

"Morning guv," says Anna cheerfully.

"Ah Anna, just the girl !"

As Anna heads for her desk, the door opens and Roger appears with a tray holding three cups and saucers and a plate of biscuits. He's clearly been to the canteen. Anna smiles to herself. Blokes getting the tea ! They are coming on in the world !

"Morning all," he grins.

The threesome gather together in a huddle. Anna is back on the case after the wolves' episode. Roger and Anna await Frank's instructions.

"Nothing much seems to be happening to help with the inquiry into Tom Preston's murder. We're going to have to go back to square one. I'd like you, Anna, to revisit Tom's parents and speak to his girlfriend again. Make sure we have a   comprehensive list of Tom's friends, people he mixed with, etc. Roger, go back to the garage where he worked. Speak to the manager, his wife and the mechanic."

Roger and Anna both nod their heads.

"I know we're going over old ground, but there has to be something we've missed.My gut instinct tells me that Tom may not be as white as he's being painted. His death wasn't a spur of the moment thing. It was planned and we want to know who by."

"I think you're right," agrees Roger. There's definitely something rotten in the state of Wanstead."

Anna looks longingly at the duo of new Panda cars in the car park. These had come into service in recent years, but were mainly used by uniformed officers whilst on urgent police duties where speed was of the esssence. The earliest of these cars had been painted black and white, hence the name 'panda'. More recently they have been painted blue and white. Each car has a radio in the car, a set which comprises a control box under the dashboard and a transmitter receiver box in the boot. Such police radio is a key way of keeping in touch and being ready to assist in any unexpected event when help is needed or in the case of an accident. Anna and Roger, however, will be using their own cars today.

Anna sets off. She decides to visit Tom's parents' house first. They live close to The Flats. His girlfriend, Mary, works during the day so Anna plans to call at her home later on. She begins by calling at the Preston's home. The house is semi-detached and situated in a quiet road. Mature trees, spilling over from the forest, line the road. It seems a very peaceful and respectable area. Anna mulls over the situation. How did a lad from such a pleasant home, with decent parents end up being the victim of a gangster ? If that is the case.

She rings the doorbell. Mrs Preston is home and quickly comes to the door. Anna notices straight away that she has been crying. She looks very tired and her body language makes her appear like a rag doll.

"I'm expecting my husband back shortly.... He's had to call in to the office." Mrs Preston says immediately on seeing Anna on the doorstep.

Is she afraid of being with me alone ? thinks Anna.

Mrs Preston anxiously takes a glance up and down the road. There's no sign of Mr Preston.

"Don't worry," Anna kindly assures the nervous woman who is hovering uncomfortably on the doorstep. " I'd just like to go over a few points with you.....May I come in ?"

Mrs Preston looks at Anna as if she's only just recognised her. "Umm, yes I suppose so dear."

She turns and walks into the hallway. Anna follows and closes the front door. It's clear Mrs Preston is upset, but is there more to that than meets the eye ? thinks Anna.

Elsie Preston escorts Anna into the living room at the front of the house. It has a bay window and is a pleasant, light, room. The furniture is old-fashioned, flower-patterned chairs and sofa adorned with cream, lace antimacassars which have been carefully ironed. The fireplace holds an electric fire with fake coals. The wooden furniture is pre-war brown and the walls papered in a flowery pattern.

"Do sit down, dear. Can I get you some tea ?"

Anna thinks that making tea might help Mrs Preston to feel more relaxed. She waits patiently, perched on the sofa, until she returns.

The tea is carried on a silver tray covered in an embroidered tea cloth. The crockery is a Willow-Pattern with cups in blue and white, as are the teapot, milk jug and sugar bowl. Mrs Preston places the tray on a small table and pours out the tea. "Milk and sugar, dear ?" she asks Anna.

"Yes please."

Anna is offered a biscuit which she refuses.

"Now how can I help you, dear…..by the way, do call me Elsie. Mrs Preston sounds so fancy."

"Thank you Elsie."

Silence follows as they each take a sip of tea.

Elsie speaks first. "Of course, you're here about Tom, aren't you, dear ?"

"That's right. I'd just like to learn more about him. I think getting to know him a little might help to give us clues about ………" Anna hesitates.

"I know," says Elsie. She pulls a handkerchief from her sleeve and wipes her eyes.

"I'm sorry to upset you, but we do want to find the truth, both from a legal point of view, but also to try and help you both to come to terms with what has happened." Anna smiles kindly at Elsie.

Elsie wipes her eyes and nods.

"Is there anything you can remember about people that Tom knew ? Did he ever imply that he was in trouble or being threatened ?"

Elsie shakes her head."You asked me that before."

" I know, but things can come to mind when you've had a chance to go over them in your head. For instance, did he go out much ? Apart from going to work I mean. You know, going to meet his friends at the pub ?"

"Not really. Since he met Mary they've always been everywhere together. Tom was never much of a lads' lad, if you know what I mean."

Anna nods. She knows she isn't getting very far. That said, she didn't want to press Elsie too much. She is clearly very fragile at present.

As Anna finishes her tea, she hears the front door opening. Moments later, Mr Preston enters the room. He looks at Anna questioningly. "Hope you're not upsetting my wife, detective !" His voice has a sharp edge to it.

Before Anna can reply, Elsie chips in. "No, she's been very kind, dear. Just trying to help solve the problem." Her voice quakes."We need to find out. To lay it to rest once and for all."

"I'm sorry to barge in, " assured Anna. "We have to find the culprit or culprits. I'm sure you want to know what happened."

Mr Preston looks annoyed. "I don't know if we do. Our son's dead and that's the end of it. You and your questions. Clear off."

Elsie quickly spoke. "Look, the young lady has a job to do. Imagine if the beast who did that, killed someone else !"

Fred Preston's face grows red. "That wouldn't be our business."

Silence ensues.

"I'm sorry to be asking you questions at this difficult time, Mr Preston, but it's my job, the police's job, to find who did this and stop them maybe doing it again. "

Fred Preston suddenly looks sad. He stares at Anna. "I know," he says slowly. "Why did it have to happen to us ?" he asks in a breaking voice. It sounds as if he is close to tears.

"Look," says Anna. "I suggest you two need to discuss this without me being here. Think hard. Anything out of the ordinary as far as Tom is concerned is of interest to us. I'll call back tomorrow……I do want to help," she adds.

Elsie shows Anna to the door. Fred Preston turns away. He doesn't look at her.

Anna is frustrated and has a bucket full of reservations about Fred Preston's attitude. Looking at her watch, she decides to head back to the station. She wants to mentally go through all the information they have so far. Hopefully, Roger may have had more success at the garage with Tony Blake or his whereabouts and amongst Tom Preston's friends. She hopes that meeting Tom's girlfriend, Mary Ryan, again may also throw some light on matters.

When Anna returns to Woodstone nick, she reports to DCI Fernbank. She explains that not much emerged and she has a feeling that Mr Preston knows something. Either he hasn't told his wife or she's keeping mum as well.

"M'mm," responds Frank. "So do you get the impression that Mrs Preston doesn't know something or that she's being forced to keep sthum ?"

"I'm not sure, but I get the impression it's just him. She may suspect something, or not, but either way, I'm convinced that facts are being kept back."

Frank thinks hard for a moment. "When Roger gets back. I suggest you organise a time for you both to visit Fred Preston at work." Frank flicks through a file. "Thought so. He works for the Post Office Sorting Office at Walthamstow. Find out when they have their lunch hour and grab him then."

"OK. Makes me wonder though, why he came home this morning."

"Probably checking on Mrs. Compassionate leave or some such. May be something or nothing, but it's worth checking."

Anna nods. "I'll go through what we know already and discuss it when Roger gets back. See if we've missed anything."

Frank nods and returns to his own office.

About 20 minutes later, Roger arrives. He regards Anna with a grin. "Short visit ?"

Anna explains what happened. "How does that seem to you ?" she asks Roger.

"M'mm. Dodgy I'd say. Let's do what Frank suggests. Pay him a little visit." Roger looks at his watch. "Midday. Bingo."

On this occasion, a 'Panda Car' is available. Roger drives and Anna follows her London street map. She gives him directions. "It's only about 15 minutes to the Sorting Office."

As usual, the traffic is heavy initially, but eases off as they head to the outskirts.

The Sorting Office is easy to find. It has only been recently opened, by Prince Charles no less. It is a strange building of metal and glass which dominates the skyline and seems out of place amongst its Victorian and pre-war neighbours.

Roger and Anna arrive in the entrance hall where there is an enquiry desk. A young woman of about Anna's age greets them. "Can I be of help ?" she asks in a rather stagey voice which sounds like a line she has learned off by heart. Roger and Anna produce their ID cards. Roger asks if he can speak to Mr Fred Preston.

"Oh, poor Mr Preston. It's such a shame. Tom is…was…a lovely chap." She looks tearful.

"You knew him ?" asks Anna.

"I did. One of my girlfriend's boyfriend, is…. was…. friends with Tom."

Anna and Roger exchange glances. "Do you have his name or a phone number ?" asks Anna.

"His name's Tony somebody. I don't know his phone number but I can get it for you."

"Phone Woodstone Police Station and speak to one of us or leave a message," says Anna. "I'm Detective Sergeant Kinsale and this…."pointing at Roger…" is Detective Inspector Edwards."

"OK. I'll do that….Anything to help catch the person responsible. The papers said it was a wild wolf attack."

"No, that's not the case," smiles Anna,"but I can't tell you any more at present. Anyway, we'd like to speak to Mr Preston briefly."

The receptionist looks puzzled. "He's not here. I believe he's been given compassionate leave. I haven't seen him in the last few days."

The two officers thank the receptionist and leave.

"So, where's he been?" asks Anna as they return to the car.

"...and," adds Roger, "could Tony be Tony Blake, the mechanic at Houghton's garage ?"

---

(12) The Patrick O'Farrell Case

No man knows the value of innocence and integrity but he who has lost them.

(William Godwin)

Anna is keen to get home. As she turns her key in the front door lock, she hears what sounds like weeping. She opens the door to the living area and discovers Philomena sitting on the sofa in floods of tears. Anna walks over to the sofa and sits on the arm of the sofa so that she can put a friendly arm around her flatmate's shoulders.

"Whatever's wrong ?" A look of concern crosses Anna's face.

Philomena hesitates and wipes her eyes on a handkerchief that Anna had proffered. "It's my brother. I visited him today and he's so depressed."

"Why's he depressed ?"

Philomena replies through sobs. "He's been in prison for a year......" She stops to wipe her eyes.

"In prison ?" It's the first Anna has heard about this.

"I'm sorry. I should have told you, but I didn't when I moved here and after that I just never seemed to find the right opportunity. I guess I worried that, as a police officer, you wouldn't want the sister of a criminal sharing your flat. Of course, I know you better now, but as time went on I just couldn't bring myself to tell the truth. In fact, if I ever had a sister it was you. You're the one who I can trust. ......I hope you can forgive me." Philomena begins to cry again.

Anna stays where she is, perched on the arm of the sofa, trying to get her head round these revelations. "Which prison is he in ?"

"Wandsworth. It's a horrible place. It was built over a hundred years ago and it's awful. Patrick, that's my brother, told me that 135 inmates were....." Philomena searches for the words.... "put to death there between 1878 and 1961. He says it has the smell of misery and death throughout. The prison officer who took him to his cell, said with a smirk, 'Welcome to your cell, chum.' When that door banged shut, he felt as if he'd been separated from the outside world forever. ....the trouble is that when prisoners are together, like in the exercise yard, they all seem to sense weakness on his part. One man whispered in his ear, 'take a look around you, mate. If you can't see the walls closing in, you soon will.' He laughed nastily. I'm scared that Patrick is in danger of ......" She pauses, wiping away a tear, "doing away with himself...."

"Can I ask why he's in prison ? Anna asks warily.

"He started working as a volunteer in a homeless charity. It's called 'Help the Homeless', helping tramps....homeless people. You know, people living outside in the streets. He'd done book-keeping work before and he was paid a small wage to keep the books. Patrick thought he was helping to sort out donations which had been collected from people in the street....you know places like Oxford Street where there are plenty of shoppers."

Anna nods.

Philomena continues. "He got to know some of the people they were helping. He joined a group of people who ran soup kitchens and he helped with those too. He liked the work. He felt he was doing something good." She pauses.

Anna nods sympathetically. "So what happened ?"

"Well, he got to know several of these homeless people. The hostel staff gave them a meal and a bed for the night. Some spent time there. Others came once in a while to have a wash and a meal.....Patrick said they didn't want to stay in the hostel for a long time. It was too regulated. Despite the problems and dangers of surviving on the streets, they seemed to want...what I suppose you'd call.... some kind of independence."

Anna thinks about her own experiences as a WPC on the streets. It's true that night shelters are places to sleep for people who would otherwise be on the streets. They don't have to pay to stay in most night shelters. Some are only open in the winter though or when there is extreme weather. The 'customers' arrive by a set time in the evening and leave in the morning.

Anna asks Philomena, "how come when Patrick was helping the homeless, he got involved in a crime ?"

"The charity that runs the 'Help the Homeless' hostel was robbed of a substantial amount of money which had come from donations. Patrick, having been given the job of bookeeper, was the first to fall under suspicion by them. The charity's trustees were convinced that the theft had been an inside job and subsequently, blame fell on Patrick. He'd been responsible for taking cash to the bank. One morning, one of the charity's organisers opened a bank statement from which it was clear that large sums of money were missing. Patrick was the obvious culprit. There wasn't another suspect and to add to the problem, it was discovered that the money disappearing coincided with the time Patrick began working for them. It seemed a clear case and Patrick was arrested, tried and sentenced to two years in prison for fraud. He'd been told by the police that the charity had generously agreed that if he returned the money he wouldn't be prosecuted. Of course, Patrick didn't have the kind of sums they were talking about. This contributed to his being found guilty."

"Patrick is so depressed in jail. He gets bullied." Philomena begins to speak hesitantly. "You remember Ronnie Biggs ? He was serving a thirty year jail sentence in Wandsworth for his part in The Great Train Robbery."

"Of course," says Anna, puzzled by this revelation.

"Well, Patrick got...what's the expression ?.... Yes, 'stitched up', that's it. By Biggs. One of Biggs' cronies spoke to Patrick one dinner time. He said that Biggs was planning to escape. He wanted Patrick to use his influence to get Ronnie Biggs a hideout underground through Patrick's work with the homeless.....Apparently," she adds tearfully, "many homeless people join groups and live underground, like in old, unused tube stations;"

Anna interrupts, " but couldn't Patrick have reported it ? "As she speaks these words, she realises how hopeless and intimidated Patrick must have felt.

Philomena nods. "He was threatened by Biggs' henchman. A big chap, Tommy someone, who intimidated Patrick with violence if he didn't comply......What Biggs wanted was a place to hide on the outside while he waited to get out of the country. He knew about the underground hideouts used by some people living on the streets, but he'd discovered that access was pretty well impossible. There were padlocked doors to gain entry, as well as closely guarded secret passwords only available to those in the homeless community who use the places."

Anna was amazed by these revelations. "So what happened ?"

Having been threatened, Patrick decided to ask for help from a friend of his who had visited him regularly in prison. He had been a fellow worker helping the homeless. I don't know his name. Patrick doesn't want me to know too much. In fact, what I have learned could have landed me in trouble with Ronnie Biggs."

"Not a man to be crossed, if I remember rightly," adds Anna, sympathetically. She could imagine what a dreadful situation Patrick would have been in.

Philomena nods. "Through this friend, whose name Patrick hasn't told me, a man was found who had access to one of the underground bases via a secret tunnel.....he wouldn't tell me any more for my own good, but this man was offered a large sum of money to help Biggs escape......Patrick told me he had been offered a chance to escape and a reward of money if things went well......he didn't want money and neither did he want to escape. There's no way he wanted to increase the time he was to spend in prison if he got caught."

Anna recalls that Biggs had served only fifteen months of his thirty year sentence before escaping from Wandsworth Prison. He had escaped from his cell somehow and then scaled the prison wall with a rope ladder and dropped onto the roof of a waiting removal van.

Philomena continues the story. "Biggs had promised to take Patrick and another man called Seabourne with him. Seabourne was to ensure that Patrick came with them, albeit reluctantly, so that he couldn't blow the whistle on the plan. However, when they reached the wall, Biggs climbed up and jumped on the vehicle's roof as arranged. Then, the van takes off leaving Patrick and Seabourne behind. They were quickly captured. They were both sentenced to another four years on top of their sentences for helping Biggs to escape."

Anna recalls mention of that situation. It was big news at the time. She hadn't known of course that Patrick was one of the pair involved.

Philomena continues. "Later, in prison, Patrick heard on the grapevine that Biggs had fled to Belgium by boat then sent a note to his wife to join him in Paris. There, he had acquired new identity papers and the rumour was that he underwent plastic surgery to disguise himself and avoid capture."

Anna recalls station gossip quite recently. Only this year, it was rumoured that Ronnie Biggs had escaped to Australia, taking with him the money from the robbery which had been hidden undiscovered during his prison sentence. Detective Chief Superintendent Leonard 'Nipper' Read of Scotland Yard had been promoted two years before to the Murder Squad. He had been involved in capturing the Great Train Robbers. Read's first assignment, in 1964, had been to bring down the notorious Kray twins. Reggie Kray, Ronnie's twin brother, was still, at that time, being investigated for a number of violent crimes. The rumour amongst the police was that Reggie was 'protected' from arrest because he was involved with some 'influential' people and his arrest could reveal things that those on high would not want revealed. Anna is realising that Patrick has been dealing with some very unsavoury and high-profile characters. The chances of him getting an early release seems unlikely at this moment in time. She doesn't say this to Philomena though.

Philomena continues. "Patrick has got a legal advisor who is trying to help him. After all, everything he did was under pressure and he knows how foolish it was to try and escape. He suffers from claustrophobia. That means he has an intense fear and anxiety about being trapped in small or enclosed spaces. People with claustrophobia can experience an intense fear of suffocation or restriction in a prison cell and the desire to escape is stronger than it might be in others. It's one reason why he took such risks....." Her eyes fill with tears......"that and the violence threatened. The solicitor doesn't charge for his services because Patrick has no income, so he's entitled to legal aid."

Anna nods. She can't help thinking though that helping such a notorious criminal as Ronnie Biggs to escape will be a strong reason not to let Patrick gain a shorter sentence.

---

(13) A Helping Hand

"A helping hand can be a ray of sunshine in a cloudy world." (anon)

Anna has decided to approach her boss, DCI Fernbank about Patrick O'Farrell's plight. She doesn't hold out much hope for a positive response, but she feels she'd like to try for her flatmate's sake.

Unfortunately, after hearing the tale, Frank Fernbank is not very hopeful for any chance of an early release for Patrick. "What the lad should have done was to report the bullying and pressure on him to the prison guards. If they'd been aware of this it might have elicited some sympathy and action."

Anna says, "but if Biggs had discovered that Patrick had reported the matter, he'd probably have punished him in a really violent way, or even had him killed. You know how things work in prison. Patrick is an innocent and he's suffering severely now for something that wasn't his fault."

"Yeah. Trouble is, Anna, as you know by now, things are never straightforward."

Anna looks as if she's going to say something, but then stops herself.

Fernbank can see how this has affected her. "You can't get embroiled in something like this, Anna. It could affect your career.....Look, tell you what, I'll have a word with this legal aid lawyer chap, see it from his point of view, but don't hold your breath."

At least that's something, thinks Anna. She decides not to mention the conversation to Philomena in case nothing comes from Frank Fernbank's enquiries. On the other hand, she decides, there's nothing to prevent her from asking a few questions to a couple of street dwellers that she knows, or even making enquiries amongst the charity staff and volunteers who help the homeless. Maybe she could find out more about these underground hideouts.

That evening, after she had clocked off, Anna goes to the 'Help the Homeless' shelter where she knows a couple of the volunteers in the soup kitchen, as well as some of the 'customers'. She knows that Patrick is only 22 years old.

One of the guys she knows is Mick. He's a similar age. He had been on the streets as a youngster and had been in trouble with the police several times for minor offences, including smoking cannabis, but he was now 'going straight'. He had 'made good' and got a job as a motorbike courier. However, he still has connections with street dwellers using the 'Help the Homeless' and mixes in their community. He could even be a useful source for finding more about Tony Blake, in terms of the drugs issue. Equally, he might be able to throw some light on Patrick O'Farrell's fate.

Anna knows that Mick and his mates gather together on part of 'The Flats'.Maybe he knows about Patrick O'Farrell. Mick is a good-looking young man with dark, slicked back hair in a Teddy Boy style. He's dressed like a 'rocker', wearing combat boots, a leather jacket decorated with metal spikes, a white scarf and blue jeans. Rockers being young motorcyclists who consider themselves outside the 'norms' of society. They are seen as intimidating by many adults who feel they display aggression, criminality and have a high alcohol consumption ! They and their motorbikes demonstrate physical strength and sometimes, not always, violence. Anna has always had a good relationship with Mick and he has proved to be a reliable 'grass'.

Anna finds Mick with a group of friends outside a pub, 'The King's Head', on the borders of The Flats. Mick is well known at the homeless shelter. The staff at the shelter know Mick as someone who wanders in just before closing-up time at 10pm. He'll have a coffee, maybe to sober up, followed by a wash and brush-up. Unfortunately, a part-time job as a courier doesn't pay much and flat rentals in London and its surrounds, even for bedsits, are beyond his pocket. Angie, one of the girls who works at the shelter, says he uses some of the money he gets from odd jobs in his spare time and 'other' sources to put his clothes through the washateria. "He takes a pride in his appearance," Angie, a volunteer at the shelter had said.

Anna finds Mick with a group of friends outside a pub, 'The King's Head', on the borders of The Flats. Like his peers, he is wearing a black leather jacket, tight blue jeans and other motorcycle-related attire. The group of Rockers are gathered outside the pub, drinking pints of beer. When Anna appears in plain clothes and approaches Mick, she gets some wolf whistles. There's lots of teasing. "Blimey, is that your new bint, Mick ?"

Mick nods confidently.

Anna has always loved 'The Flats'. Its vast open space stretches like the sort of green garden interspersed with trees that might surround a stately home or a grand house in the suburbs. The Flats are, like many of its inhabitants untamed for the most part, but in places mown and managed like a public park. Every day, a range of people visit. Runners, dog walkers, tourists and bird-lovers looking out for signs of avian residents amongst the trees. Even kestrals are not unknown here. In the school summer holidays, a travelling circus or a fairground will appear. Summer also brings sunbathers, picnicking families, footballers and groups of teenagers laughing and joking. In the winter, when it snows, people arrive with toboggans which are used on the slight slopes to be found on the boundaries.

Anna knows that homeless people sometimes sleep rough in the scrub. They clear a well-hidden spot where they pitch their makeshift tents amongst the bushes after dark. There are many such people who for many different reasons do not have homes to return to. London rents and property prices being so high and out of the reach of many. Social housing is often just out of reach and many people remain on council properties' lists for over a year or more.

Anna knows that there has never been an accurate count of homeless people. They are often invisible, forgotten by society and its norms. The police know that the homeless exist in hundreds, even thousands. There are efforts towards creating an annual census of rough sleepers. Volunteers carry out head counts, but this is often only by a show of hands. There's a vast population that cannot be accounted for. One of the volunteers had once told Anna "You could be next to someone in a pub or a cafe, an art gallery or a shop and not know that the person was homeless." Charities regularly try to draw attention to the complicated problem of what might be called 'hidden homelessness'. People who are not counted and may well not want to become a statistic. One charity volunteer had spoken to Anna and referred to 'a grey world'. People being invisible as if they are an integral component of the smog which drifts in from city traffic and chimneys.

Anna ignores the teasing. The other bikers finish their drinks and prepare to leave. Mick stays behind, which initiates more teasing as they depart. Once they've gone, Anna sits with Mick and she orders them both a drink. A pint for him and a shandy for Anna. She begins by asking him about the charity 'Help the Homeless'. He knows about what happened to Patrick and explains to her that he feels there was something dodgy about the whole thing.

"What do you mean ?" asks Anna.

"I think the bloke who runs 'Help the Homeless', is a con artist."

"Why do you say that ?"

"I dunno. Not sure who's kosher or not there, but someone is a bleedin' magician that's what. There's one or more light-fingered buggers working there. Blokes, there're not many female tramps, are encouraged to strip off, take a bath. Often they're paralytic. Don't know their arses from their elbows....sorry Miss, er Sergeant...."

"No offence taken," grins Anna. "Go on."

"Some of these homeless blokes collect a tidy sum. A lot goes on booze or maybe drugs. They have secret pockets in their coats. When they're getting a wash, or sleeping, one or more of the so-called 'helpers' will help themselves. They always leave a bit to ensure that the bloke won't get suspicious.... It ain't right, is it ?

"No," agrees Anna, deep in thought. "So was Patrick involved in the thefts ?"

"No, that's the thing. There was a fella called Jack. He was quite old. Maybe 50....."

Anna knows that 50 seems old to young people, but being homeless does age people very quickly.

"This Jack, he was careful with his money. It was rumoured that he had a fortune tucked away in his bag. He never let go of that bag, always round his neck.....One night, he wakes up to find most of the money from the bag had been nicked. He was all right up there, you know." Mick taps the side of his head. "Well, he made a hell of a stink. Called them thieves. It was Patrick's bad luck that he was the newest recruit to the team. He immediately got the blame from the real culprit or culprits. Everyone reckoned someone, or maybe more than one, had fiddled the books and Patrick was the ideal patsy. It was the manager, John Lincoln, who gave Patrick the push."

"M'mm. What sort of a character is Lincoln ?"

"Well, he plays the part of the caring person really well, especially in front of people he wants to impress. Wears suits from Savile Row. Thinks he's the business ! He puts himself over as having good intentions and being big hearted. We all know that's crap. He has dodgy intentions. He's creepy. You know, pretends to be your mate, but it's all an act. Yeah, he gives me the creeps. In fact...." Mick pauses. 'There is even talk of him being involved in drugs. You know selling them to addicts who visit the shelter. It's even said that he uses some of the younger lads as runners. Give them drugs in return for selling them on. I don't like to think what could happen if he found out anyone was cheating him."

This is news to Anna and her mind is whirling with this important information."M'mm, going back to the theft, why didn't you speak to Patrick's lawyer, or even the police at the time ?"

"I didn't wanna get involved. Poking your nose in could mean getting beaten up or worse. If he done what he did to Patrick, gawd knows what he'd do to the likes of me ! "

Anna nods sympathetically. She is pleased at Mick's news. She has to report it to the boss and see if anything can be done for Patrick. The possible drugs connection certainly needed investigation.

"Look," says Mick, I ain't getting too involved in this. My mates'll get suspicious."

Anna thanks him, gives him five pounds for his trouble. (hoping Frank will see fit to refund her) They part and she walks away. So, the plot thickens, she thinks.

---

(14) Living Underground

'You've made your bed, you better lie in it

You choose your leaders and place your trust

As their lies wash you down and their promises rust

You'll see kidney machines replaced by rockets and guns

And the public wants what the public gets

But I don't get what this society wants

I'm going underground.'

(The Jam, 1980)

Anna had been finding out more about the invisible homeless who live just a few feet beneath some of London's busiest roads. Its communities of homeless people who are living in conditions most people couldn't even imagine. In fact, she learned that the vast majority of thousands of pedestrians walking through London's streets every day will have no idea about the existence endured by those living underneath their feet. They are the city's hidden homeless who have made a form of home for themselves.

She asks her boss, Frank Fernbank, about these people.

"Yes, it's true, They call it 'going underground'. It's a precarious existence, but hidden away from society's gaze."

Fernbank describes how only recently, two youngsters aged 15 and 16, a boy and a girl, had been discovered asleep under blankets on the remains of a black leather sofa on the Mile End underpass. "The lad had been badly beaten up trying to protect his girlfriend when a couple of yobs found them and laid into them. They kicked the lad and planned to assault the girl. The lad had a knife which he used to threaten them and after a while they thought better of it and left. Those two were lucky. A PC on patrol had heard the altercation and went to investigate. The youngsters refused to say much."

Anna is shocked. "What happened ?"

"PC Jones brought them to the station. They have been taken into care...." Frank sighs. "Trouble is, it won't be long before they do a runner and start their street life again."

Frank continues. "Apparently, they were lying just inches from the water's edge behind two metal barriers perched beside the running water and supported by concrete blocks. It's incredibly precarious. What few, sorry possessions they did have were kept neatly in a tatty old suitcase. The floor was littered with broken bottles, tin cans and food....They weren't very keen to come to the station with us."

'We won't live like people live on the streets,' said the lad. 'We have a sofa and bedding, it's very comfortable.' "God, the optimism of the young ! The girl had explained that they both showered three times a week at a hostel for the homeless. It's a shame. I think of my own kids and can't begin to imagine them in that situation. That dark, dingy tunnel is their home."

Anna says that she had heard there were many such places, including old, unused tunnels and stations on the London Underground train system.

"The thing is that living in this secluded tunnel, close to the City's intricate canal system, Charlie and June stay dry and relatively warm. Hidden from the world they believe they are safe there. It's heartbreaking."

Anna nods solemnly. "I remember a case recently, which was awful. A member of the public reported that a homeless man had been sleeping on a perilously narrow ledge only twenty feet above the River. Apparently, he had to press himself right up against the wall in a bid to stop himself falling into the water."

Fernbank nods. "I remember it. A journalist from The Daily Mirror heard about it and managed to get a photo of the man in situ."

Anna nodded sadly. "It does highlight the stark reality of life for many homeless people on the streets."

'Yes, and they are in danger because people sleeping rough have been deliberately hit or kicked or experienced some other form of violence. It's likely why that particular bloke was risking his life by sleeping in a potentially dangerous location in a bid to keep away from others."

."What a world," muses Anna. She tells Frank about the suspicions of Mick, a part-time user of the Help the Homeless' hostel.

"Tell you what, visit the Help the Homeless hostel yourself to see what you can find out . Maybe we can find out more about these underground bods and see if we can find any info about drug dealing."

Anna is pleased to be on the tracks and moving towards the uncovering of possible financial fraud and the drugs trade being operated from the Help the Homeless hostel. John Lincoln, the Manager, could well be up to no good, despite his outward appearance of being a carer to those in need.

···

Danny Smith is 18 years old. He'd been brought up in a children's home after being discarded by his mother when he was just a baby. At 14 he'd run away from the children's home, tired of their treatment of youngsters with their strict rules as well as corporal punishments being a daily occurrence. He'd survived outdoors and in hostels since then. He had started taking drugs the previous year. He is now is trying to stop and is now almost 'clean'. He now wants to go somewhere where he can resist temptation.

Going to the 'Help the Homeless' place had proved to be a big mistake. When the person running the bloody place starts dealing drugs, Danny thought, it's the end. He's seen what happens to long-term drug users. He hates John Lincoln with a vengeance. As rumour has it, he's nicking money from some of the hostel's 'customers' and even from the hostel organisation itself. Clever thing is, he knows none of the homeless blokes will report theft of money or admit to buying drugs, or dealing them, through the hostel's own manager !

A while ago Danny had discovered a homeless community living around the place called 'The Flats'. He had learned the history of the area from one of the old blokes at the hostel. Apparently, this large piece of open land has been used as a hideout or resting place for centuries. People in flight from plague camped here in the 17th century, as did preachers, passing travellers and highwaymen. Danny had heard the story of the infamous Dick Turpin. Some criminals had been hanged here, too. In medieval times there was said to have been wolves roaming free. Gardeners were allowed to dig allotments here during the First World War, and in World War Two, The Flats were commandeered for the testing of anti-aircraft guns.

Homeless people had long become familiar figures around the hidden places amongst the trees and brambles. The neighbours constantly complain loudly to the Council and the police. However, for a long time, rough sleepers on The Flats had simply been ushered away, preferably over the other side of borough lines, to become somebody else's problem.

The police were always nearby waiting for the right time to find homeless people and move them on, hopefully in the direction of help from hostels, not just onto another patch of land for rough camping. Danny thought it was mean and unfair that often the police or council officials would wait until winter to do this. In the winter the scrub became sparser and easier to look for, and spot, rough camps. Winter was also a time for council workmen to plunge in and clear up litter and other unexpected items that got left behind – large items like old prams, empty beer and drink bottles and sometimes old munitions ! Over the years, they had even discovered bodies on the heath, both murder victims and suicides.

Danny had become very aware that even though rough camp homes offered pretty poor protection from the weather or those trying to attack rough sleepers, these paltry places, nevertheless, offered safety, sanctuary, a sense of putting down roots and even, to some extent at least, control over their own lives. Homeless people often felt safer in small groups. That said, Danny knew that those who are dependent on drugs or alcohol, tended to stay on the periphery of such groups.

In addition to places like The Flats, Danny had heard rumours about numerous underground communities of homeless people. He is now seeking a new place to rest his head. Before he had discovered more about the 'Underground' shelters that some homeless people used, young Danny was, himself, living in a hideout on The Flats. One night he had been to the Help the Homeless hostel to have something to eat and a warm shower. Once he'd decided to try and wean himself off cannabis, he had discovered that John Lincoln usually left the hostel around 5ish, so if he arrived later, he'd miss him and keep out of temptation's way. This evening it was dark by the time he'd left the hostel to make his way back to the camp on The Flats.

Approaching the camp he collides with what he recognises as a crime scene. There are police cars and vans in The Flats' car park and uniformed officers who are forming a long, snaking cordon that encircles his camp. Danny squats down, hiding behind some bushes, watching what is going on. Around only twelve feet or so ahead police have erected a large white tent. They have brought in dogs. Both plain-clothed detectives and uniformed officers are searching the area and conversing in groups. To one side stand several of his homeless comrades who have been disturbed.

Danny knows the police dogs could soon catch his scent. He walks out from his hiding place and approaches the cordon. He begins calling to a non-existent dog. "Here Pluto. Where are you, boy ?"

He is stopped by a uniformed constable. "You can't come any closer mate."

"What's going on ?" asks Danny. He can see there are officers from neighbouring boroughs. Far more than would be needed to move along a few stubborn homeless people.

"You can't come through here," repeats the constable.

"Have you seen my dog ?" asks Danny cheekily.

The constable doesn't reply, simply turns his back.

Danny retraces his steps, cutting across the darkened heath to the bank of a large pond, where he finds a fellow camper, Dennis, on their usual park bench.

"What's all this bollocks about?" asks Danny.

Dennis shrugs his shoulders. "Dunno mate. I'm keeping well clear."

They both agree it didn't look promising. Dennis reaches into his coat and produces a can of beer. They share a last beer together, then go their separate ways. Danny isn't too worried. He has other places he can sleep. He had discovered a carpeted corner in the entrance to a bank. He had been sheltering in the entrance way outside when, one particularly cold winter's evening, a sympathetic caretaker had invited him inside. He now makes his way there. As he rests inside in his sleeping bag, with a welcome cup of tea, he keeps thinking about the scale of the crime scene.

The next morning Danny buys a newspaper from a nearby news-stand. The body of a young man had been discovered on The Flats. So far he had not been identified. It seemed that several homeless men had made a camp in the area. They had been taken into custody for interrogation.

Danny decides to lie low and not return to the camp for a while, if at all. The investigation could go on for months.

The following day, Danny pulls a newspaper out of a bin. He is concerned to read that the identity of the victim on The Flats had not yet been discovered. The newspaper states that police are searching for a young man who had crossed the area of The Flats where the crime took place and had, apparently, been searching for a lost dog. Police are anxious to speak to this man in case he had seen anything.

Danny wakes up hungry, so decides to call in at the Help for the Homeless hostel to have a clean-up and something to eat. As he enters, he spots Mick the Biker, tucking into a fried breakfast of eggs and bacon. Danny nods to him and after collecting his food and a cup of tea from the counter, he joins Mick.

"All right mate ?" asks Mick.

"Yeah, not bad," responds Danny.

For a few moments they each concentrate on their meal in silence. There's a slice of toast too ,spread with marg and marmalade and a mug of tea.

Danny explains what had happened on The Flats and explains how he needs to find a more permanent 'home'. He mentions underground shelters. Mick suggests he could try and go 'underground'. He advises him that he should speak to Des, another homeless young man who Mick was sure had found an underground community to live in.

As luck would have it, as Mick and Danny finish their breakfast, another young man arrives at the counter for a breakfast. He is tall and skinny with dark blonde hair. As he walks away with his tray of food, Mick calls him over and invites him to sit with him and Danny. He introduces Danny to Des.

"Danny's had a problem with his camp on The Flats," explains Mick, speaking in hushed tones. "Do you reckon you could help him get underground ?"

Des studies Danny, who notices Des's deep blue eyes staring at him as if sussing him out. "I can try. Let me have my nosh and I'll take him over."

Mick says goodbye and leaves the two men together. There's silence while they both finish their meal. Danny waits for Des to drink his tea.

"I'll leave," says Des conspiratorially. "Give me five minutes and I'll meet you round the corner on the bench near the tobacconists."

Danny does as he's asked. When they meet up, Danny finds himself taken by Des to what he discovers is Wood Lane, a disused London Underground station. It had fallen into disuse in 1959. Des explains how over the following years, the platforms had gradually been taken over by homeless people. They had formed their own community, looking out for one another and deterring entry by those outside the group. On the platforms there was space for quite a few camp beds, all pushed against opposite walls. Even along the unused tracks there was ample head height. The walls were tiled and remains of old notices and advertisements were still visible. Some residents had put up hooks for clothing as well as for bags with personal belongings and even some cooking utensils. There was an unwritten agreement that nobody stole from any other. Makeshift shelves had been erected for odds and ends. There was even a portable calor gas stove down here and a couple of paraffin heaters. A large saucepan released the smell of soup cooking in a pan. A shared repas. After eating, any litter was placed inside waste bags, to be spirited away to a distant bin early the next morning. Even washing up was possible due to some nifty handiwork to open a water pipe running through the station and fill up water cans.

Danny is amazed and excited about the possibility of living in such a community.

When they arrive at Wood Lane underground station Des pulls out a key and opens a sturdy-looking padlock on a solid wooden door. Another sturdy locked door awaits them. Des knocks on the internal door. Des and Danny wait. Soon a voice can be heard from the other side of the door.

"Password ?" growls a deep voice.

"Shoreditch," says Des confidently, holding his face close to the door.

This time the two men hear bolts being drawn across. Standing inside the door is a older man. He is dressed scruffily, and strangely, in Danny's view, wearing a pair of wellington boots.

The man looks questionally at Des and then supiciously at Danny. "Who's he ?" he asks.

"This is Danny. He's all right Harry. Honest. I met him at the hostel. Thought you could help him."

"Why would I want to do that ?" asks Harry gruffly.

"He had a place in a camp on The Flats, but it's riddled with coppers now. Reckon someone's snuffed it. It's a crime scene now, so Danny don't want to go back."

"H'mm," is Harry's response. Nevertheless, he ushers them both inside and shuts and rebolts the door.

To Danny's amazement, they descend to what was clearly an underground trainline platform. As Des had described, the peeling walls still bear the remains of Underground train route maps and advertisements on large placards. He's amazed to find a seemingly well-organised group living there. There are camp beds on the platform on one side of the track. On the opposite platform is a motley collection of old chairs and tables, even some cupboards.

Only two older men are present. Danny assumes that the others must return to the surface during the day. Harry introduces him to Jack. Des and Danny are told to stay put while Harry and Jack move along the platform, deep in conversation. After a while they return.

Harry speaks. "After some discussion we're accepting you on probation."

"We'll give you a chance," says the one known as Jack, who has a grisly beard and wears an old overcoat which has seen better days. "Ever taken drugs ?"

Danny finds himself blushing. He decides to tell the truth. "I did take cannabis for a while, but nothing stronger. I'm clean now. Honest."

"Harry speaks in a deep, croaky voice. "We have had some come here that are trying to wean themselves off drugs. They have to follow our rules. We'll help them go 'cold turkey'.

Danny knew what this meant.

You might be useful to help some of the addicts we have here."

Danny nods enthusiastically.

"If you follow the rules and keep your head down when out on the streets, you will be accepted as a member of the community and issued with your own precious padlock key, which you guard with your life. The password is changed every day. Make sure you know it in the morning or you won't be allowed back in. You keep schtum about this location to anyone outside the community. In the meantime, for now, you will accompany Des in and out and arrange to meet up with him at the end of a day so that you can return to Wood Lane together."

Danny nods solemnly. Whilst on the streets, he had always feared that his eventual discovery was inevitable. He now knew that, as long as he observed the community's precautions, the outcome could be deferred for an improbable length of time.

So, he concentrates so as to remind himself of the main rules that he is being told.

    (1) Not to mention the hideout to anyone outside.
    (2) Not to leave giveaway litter in the street above.
    (3) No lingering near the outside door during daylight hours.
    (4) If someone turns up pissed or high on drugs they will be denied entry.

Danny keeps his meagre possessions in his large rucksack which he always carries with him. He also has his guitar. He understands from Jack that here, his belongings are to be considered 'temporary'. Anything valuable which gets stolen, confiscated, or trashed is down to Danny.

Finally, Danny is told that for the first few nights he must come back after dark with Des. Once he has proved himself trustworthy he will get his own key to the outside padlock. Danny leaves the underground shelter with Des and they make their way together back to the local town centre where they split up and agree to meet up for an evening meal and a bath at the Help the Homeless hostel.

Danny keeps away from The Flats for the rest of the day. One of his few treasured possessions is his guitar. Everyday he busks in the square, close to the 'The Cozy Cafe'. Sometimes, he's even invited in to play and sing. He prides himself on his musical abilities.

Danny too had known Patrick O'Farrell and what had happened to him. Danny had liked Patrick and believed that he had been the victim of the so-called charity's boss. Danny decides to keep his ear to the ground in case he can find anything about what happened.

Danny waits until the evening before finding his way back to the hostel. When he arrives there's no sign of Des. He queues up for his evening meal - corned beef, mashed potatoes and chopped beetroot. There's a custard tart for afters. A large mug of tea is also placed on his tray. The lady serving him, Molly, has a soft spot for Danny and sneaks him two custard tarts - his favourite !

Just as he finishes his breakfast, a lady walks in. She's a bit older than him. In her twenties, certainly attractive and well-dressed. She clearly is not homeless. Danny earwigs as she speaks to the man in charge that day, Ronald Peston, one of the senior volunteers, who was in conversation with a fellow female volunteer, whose name Danny didn't know.

Danny gets up from the table where he has been eating and wanders over to be close to where the lady is speaking. He puts his knapsack down closer to the pair and pretends to fiddle around with the contents as a ploy to earwig on what is being said. He soon learns that the pretty lady's name is

Philomena O'Farrell and she is making enquiries about her brother, Patrick, who she knew had worked at the hostel. Danny immediately thinks of John Lincoln, the slimeball manager of the hostel, who had sacked Patrick and reported him to the police. Lincoln had always played the part of the concerned carer. Danny's pretty sure it was all an act. He had discovered that other hostel users felt the same. The way Lincoln grovelled to the police or other officials and visitors makes him sick. He wouldn't trust the bloke further than he could throw him. Danny hadn't seen him recently. He's convinced that Lincoln was involved in Patrick's downfall. He'd used Patrick as a patsy. Danny forms a plan in his mind. If he leaves the hostel now and then lurks close to the entrance, he can catch the lady on her way out. He'd put the cat among the pigeons all right.

---

(15) Innocent But Found Guilty?

The trust of the innocent is the liar's most useful tool. (anon)

Back at the police station, after the wolves' incident, Frank Fernbank approaches Anna and Roger as they are writing up their respective notes on the matter.

"Roger, I don't know if you are aware of a situation which has come to my attention through Anna." He nods at Anna, then asks her to explain what she knows about the case of Patrick O'Farrell.

Anna gives a brief resume as she remembers it. "OK, well the case wasn't dealt with by us, but by Stratford station. Of course, Murray's in charge there now", she says smiling.

Fernbank adds, "Yeah well, the DCI who preceded him headed the team who were involved in the arrest and detention of one Patrick O'Farrell."

"I remember the case," nods Roger. "He was found guilty of cooking the books at some homeless shelter where he worked. Bit of a rotten thing to do as those places rely on charity donations."

Anna opens her mouth to pitch into the discussion, but Frank gives her a look and carries on. "Well it seems that this O'Farrell bloke may have been wrongly convicted. His sister has been working to set up a campaign for a further investigation into the matter. It seems that further information may have come to light to suggest it was, in fact, another person working at the hostel who was responsible."

"Who's your informant ?" asks Roger. "I presume one of the residents at the shelter has spoken out, although that seems unlikely knowing the members of the homeless community. Thought they avoid contact with us lot if they can."

"That's true," agrees Frank. He can see Anna is bursting to chip in. "Come on then Anna, you explain."

"The man's name is Patrick O'Farrell. I know about the situation......because my flatmate, Philomena O'Farrell, it turns out, is the sister of the accused." Anna comes to a dramatic halt.

"Wow !" says Roger. "and she wants you....well, us....to get involved ?" He looks tentatively at Frank Fernbank to gauge his reaction.

Frank steps in. "I'm having some bobbies on the beat, in the area of the hostel, to keep an ear open and see if any gems of information come to light. It does seem though that Patrick was well-regarded by many of the hostel's customers. Most were surprised when O'Farrell was arrested. Rumour has it that the lad was set up, possibly by the manager of the hostel, one John Lincoln. Bit of a slippery character by all account."

Anna is pleased to hear these revelations. It suggests that her boss is taking the matter seriously.

"I may be wrong, but copper's instinct suggests there could be something in it. Anna, now we've sorted the wolves' issue, I'd like you to speak again to your flat-mate. Don't promise her anything, but just see if she can give us any clues which might help. Roger, I'd like you to arrange a prison visit to go and speak to Patrick O'Farrell. You're just a mate of his. Don't want any prisoners thinking the bloke's helping us. Get his side of the story. I'll fish out the paperwork on the case."

Anna beams. "Thanks boss."

Anna and Roger wait for a moment.

"Get to it then, the pair of you," grins Fernbank as he leaves the room.

(16) Danny meets Philomena

"A journey of a thousand miles begins with a single step." (Lao Tzu, semi-legendary ancient Chinese Taoist philosopher)

Danny is learning a lot about life in the tunnel. He remembers reading a book, during one of his short spells at school, called 'Lord of the Flies.' It tells the story of a group of boys who find themselves alone on a desert island. They develop rules and a system of organization. They see themselves as belonging to a kind of brotherhood or tribe. However, as the story unfolds they each become threatened by violence from the others. At least at Wood Lane, thinks Danny, there are peacekeepers who are not slow in chucking out anyone threatening violence or stealing from others.

As a new boy to life underground, he still finds it incredible. He thinks to himself how you don't realise how you're slowly dropping down into a different world, operating by different rules from the world above. Danny thinks about his life since being on the streets. He guesses that you don't notice the fall from society above ground because you get used to each lower level. By the time he has now made the move underground, it's giving him a sense of relief. It was like having his own place. His life in the dark interior of the labyrinth, means he is safe from the police and those who might cause him harm up on the streets. They never come down here. Returning from the streets each day is like coming home and closing the front door. It gives him a welcome security. For Danny, the worst part of living on the surface is the feeling of being lost. Everything seems unpredictable and random. Returning to the underground at night seems like being granted a more normal life. It has a routine and that gives him security of mind. He's also discovered that the 'no drugs' rule has been bent in a good way. He's pleased that young people, like himself, who have been addicts or been tempted by drugs, or the money that can be made from selling and delivering drugs, have been allowed entry if they agree to work hard to kick the habit. Some others, who have managed to get off drugs, can remain in the security of the underground, in return for helping other addicts. It sounds easy, but Danny knows how hard it really is. He's been helping a young lad called Karl, who's only 16. Karl had left home in rural Yorkshire to find the bright lights. He'd soon been offered a job as a drug runner and from there to addiction. Danny had persuaded the underground community's leaders to allow Karl to be helped by getting him weaned off cannabis before he hit the hard drugs. Especially as Danny himself had been in that situation.

Now, he is back on the streets waiting for Philomena O'Farrell, who he knows is Patrick's sister, to leave the hostel. He plans to follow her. He waits a short distance away, pretending to look in a shop window so as not to look suspicious. Shortly afterwards, Philomena leaves the hostel and turns left. For a few minutes Danny follows her, keeping his distance. Once they are around the corner and out of sight of the hostel, Danny comes alongside Philomena. She stops, looking worried.

"I don't mean you any harm," Danny assures her quickly. "I want to tell you about Patrick."

Philomena comes unwillingly to a halt. "You know my brother ?"

"Yeah," replies Danny quickly. "I met him at the hostel. I'm one of the 'customers'. I liked Patrick. I was sorry about what happened to him." He pauses and waits to see her reaction.

Philomena looks him up and down. He is scruffily dressed, but seems genuine in what he is telling her. "Would you like a coffee ?" she asks Danny.

He hesitates. "Er, yeah, I guess."

"I'll pay," says Philomena. "Please come. I'd be grateful for any information which could help my brother."

"There's a place just up here," suggests Danny.

Philomena looks in the direction he is pointing and sees a workman's cafe, named Cozy Cafe. "OK", she says.

They enter the cafe, getting a few puzzled glances from the existing customers.

"'It's OK," says Danny. "They know me here." He looks at the woman serving behind the counter. "Two coffees please, Mavis."

Mavis is a plump, middle-aged lady with a seemingly jolly disposition. She grins and looks at Philomena as if confirming that she's paying. Philomena nods smilingly.

"Would you like a cake or a bun, Danny ?" asks Philomena.

Before Danny can reply, Mavis chips in with, "his favourites are the sticky buns." She turns to Danny "aren't they son ?"

Danny looks embarrassed and simply nods.

"Sit down dears and I'll bring 'em over," says Mavis, winking at Danny, making him blush.

There's a tense pause while they wait. As soon as Danny gets his drink and food, he scoffs the bun quickly. Philomena smiles to himself. He seems so young. She can't help wondering about his story and how he ended up homeless. However, she realises this is not the time to start being too nosey.

Anna waits for him to finish eating and then begins. "Tell me what you know about my brother and what happened to him.....please," she adds.

Danny explains his suspicions about John Lincoln, the manager of the hostel. He has decided not to mention drugs as this might confuse things. God knows what would happen if Lincoln suspected him of telling tales. "I reckon he's been getting away with it for some time. Several of us have our suspicions but he's dead crafty. He knows most of us don't want to get involved with the law. We've all been in trouble at one time or another, so we keep our heads down, 'specially those like me that are trying to go straight. I try and get work, casual labour like. It's sometimes hard because people are reluctant to give us a chance." He raises his head high. "I do my best to stay clean. Honest."

"I'm sure you do, Danny. So what can you tell me ?"

"Well, the hostel, 'Help the Homeless' is registered as a charity. People think when they donate money to the charity it'll be spent on the people it's intended for. You know, the homeless. Don't ask me how he does it, but we reckon that Lincoln, the Manager, maybe with at least one of the others, probably only spends maybe as little as 10% of donations on the homeless. He bumps up the prices he's supposed to pay for stuff like staff, food and drink and that. It's not what people expect when they drop money in a tin meant for helping the bleedin' homeless."

Danny's face is flushed and he looks angry.

Philomena looks horrified. "That's awful. Has it been reported to the police ?"

"That's the problem," explains Danny. "The likes of us aren't to be believed. Most wouldn't touch the coppers with a bargepole anyway. We reckon Lincoln cooks the books to make it all look kosher. "

"But I can't see my brother getting involved in something like that. He just wouldn't." Philomena feels her own anger rising.

Danny leans towards Philomena confidentially. "Yeah, reckon Lincoln and maybe his deputy are in it together. They pocket the donations. So when poor old Patrick is given donated amounts they're wrong anyhow. On top of that too, as I say, they make out that everything costs them more than it does. Hey Presto it all seems OK on the surface."

"That's terrible."

Danny nervously looks round before he speaks again. "Not only that, but they have been known to nick money from the 'customers' as well. A homeless bloke begs in the street and collects his donations. Some of these guys are drunks or drug addicts. When they turn up at the hostel for a meal or a wash, it's easy to pinch money from them when they're sleeping or totally out of it."

"Would you go to the police with this ?"

Danny shakes his head vehemently. "Sorry, no way."

"If I go to the police and explain I've heard about this anonymously, would that set the ball rolling ?"

"I doubt it. They've got to have proof. It's how Patrick got stitched up."

"If I go to the police, I promise not to reveal who told me."

"Try it," says Danny doubtfully.

"I'll see what I can do. I promise I won't give them your name, OK ?"

Danny shrugs. "Yeah, I guess so." He hurriedly finishes his drink, then gets up and disappears out of the door.

Philomena sits, finishing her coffee and wondering what to do. She decides she'll speak to Anna first.

(17) The Missing Tony Blake ?

If you're doing nothing wrong, you have nothing to hide. (anon)

Anna and Roger have to search to find Tony Blake. They need to find his contacts and check his movements prior to his disappearance. Frank has also suggested that they stake out the empty house they visited. Both Anna and Roger know that surveillance, being the close observation of a person or place in order to gather information, can be boring, but effective. Police forces throughout the country have found that surveillance is one of the most effective and often-used tools for monitoring criminals. If successful, it can result in invaluable information that can be used in subsequent criminal investigations or legal proceedings.

One of the most important rules, Anna has learnt, is that the police officers carrying out the surveillance have to blend in with the local environment and keep their distance, yet at the same time being close enough to catch the person and take them into custody. Parking a private car where they can see the property they hope that the criminal, in this case, Tony Blake, will return to the empty house.

Another activity is what is known as 'passive surveillance'. In this case, this includes going over information already collected to ensure that nothing has been missed. Both Anna and Roger know that comparing each other's notes of observations or interactions with a suspect is a critical practice to develop as well. Even small observations can provide useful insights into a case. For example, a simple observation of any life in the house being observed. Whether lights are on, curtains are drawn or a car is parked in a driveway can combine with other information to paint a more detailed picture of a situation.

Most importantly, Anna has learnt that in any investigation,officers must remain flexible and adaptive to any particular situation. Each surveillance situation is different and may require a different tactic or technique. Being open to change makes someone a more effective investigator and, ultimately, improves the quality of an officer's surveillance activities.

In the meantime, before this stakeout, they have also been interviewing anyone they have tracked down who knows Blake or has had dealings with him. Unfortunately this has pretty well drawn a blank. A stakeout often means backache and long hours of tense boredom, especially at night. In his frustration tonight, Roger keeps tapping the dashboard in an ever quickening pace until Anna playfully slaps his hand.

"Just stop it." She grins and passes him a bag of lemon drops.

He takes one and manages a smile. "Thanks."

The brown paper crinkles as he grasps the bag. Having helped himself to a sweet, he then releases a long sigh. Moments later, Anna notices Roger staring more closely into the darkness. "There's something", he whispers. "I'm sure I caught sight of a shadow."

Anna opens her eyes wide and stares into the darkness. Roger glances her way just long enough to see that she too is staring at something. Following her gaze, he makes out the shape of a man who appears to be dressed in black. His head is adorned with a black balacava.

"Rather overdressed for a summer's night," comments Roger.

Anna knows the moment has come. The stakeout is over. The suspect has arrived. Neither Roger nor Anna thought that Blake was likely to return to the house which they had discovered looked as if it had been empty for a while. The shadow squeezes his way past the broken front door. It seems the electric supply has been turned off because no lights have been turned on. That said, the figure must be carrying a torch because a small beam of light becomes visible in the hallway.

Roger and Anna leave the car as soon as the figure has entered the house. Roger pushes his way through the broken front door. Anna walks round the side of the house. There is no fencing and she quickly reaches the back door.

She hears Roger's voice identifying himself as the police. Anna prepares herself in case the suspect tries to escape through the back door. She hears a scuffle and pushes her way quickly through the open door. Roger has pushed the man with his front against the wall and is holding him tightly. Anna hurries forward, instructs him to put his hands behind his back and then places handcuffs on his wrists.

Roger reads the man, who they recognise as Tony Blake, his rights, explaining that he is being arrested as it is believed that he has been dealing drugs and could be involved in the murder of Thomas Preston. Blake is told he is to be taken to Woodstone Police Station where he will be held in custody in a cell and then questioned.

Roger adds, "once this procedure has been completed, you may be released or charged with a crime or crimes, as I have outlined to you."

Blake doesn't speak. He is bundled into the back of the police car and driven to the station.

(18) A Visit to Patrick

"Keep going. Better is on the way !" (anon)

Philomena arrives home in a state of anxiety. What will Anna think ? Will she trust information coming from Danny, or rather an anonymous source ? Philomena intends to keep Danny's name out of it as she promised. If she can show she's kept her word then maybe Danny will be more forthcoming on a second meeting. Maybe he could try and get hold of some proof, although that seems unlikely in his position.

As Philomena boils the kettle for a cup of tea, she hears Anna returning. She offers her a cup of tea, which Anna accepts gratefully.

"Any news about Patrick ?" asks Philomena, trying to sound casual but not succeeding.

"I can't tell you too much. I'm sure you appreciate, but let's just say wheels are in motion. Keep that strictly to yourself," Anna tells her flatmate. "You have to leave it to us. If and when you visit your brother, say nothing about police involvement. Walls have ears, especially in prison. A careless word during a visit from you could backfire and put Patrick in danger. Do you understand ?" Anna looks serious as she speaks and makes eye contact with Philomena.

"No, no, I understand," is the response. "The last thing I want to do is to endanger my brother's life." She hesitates. "Look, Anna, just between you and me, I met someone from the homeless community today. I can't tell you his name because I promised not to, but he is convinced that the manager of the Help the Homeless is up to no good, filtering donations away. He may be acting alone or with another person, but my contact isn't sure."

Anna raises her eyebrows, while Philomena takes a sip of tea. Anna realises she can't reveal any police investigation into the matter. "The thing is..." she explains to Philomena, "is that if your contact is right, he would need more than a shared suspicion without some concrete evidence." Anna then thinks quickly. "Have you arranged to see this bloke again ?"

"Not as such."

"Maybe you can arrange a meeting. Hang around where you met him before. It may well be home territory....you know somewhere he begs for money or just hangs out."

"I can try," says Philomena, "I don't think he wants to be seen talking with me. If anyone recognised me it could mean trouble for him."

"Maybe you can just walk through the area where you think he might be. Don't make contact, but make sure he sees you. If he's got any nouse, he'll maybe move off and he can follow you – at a distance of course."

Anna knows that Roger is going to meet Philomena's brother, Patrick, in prison. Maybe he can elicit some more information about the fraud. If that's the case then she's sure that their boss, Frank Fernbank, will take further action. She doesn't question Philomena any more, but she's determined to find out more than she already knows about the fraud and how the police will continue to deal with it. She plans to do her own research.

....

A week later, Philomena visits Patrick in prison. She is shocked when he is brought into the visitors' room. He has lost weight and has a greyish pallor to his skin. She's sure he hasn't been sleeping. He gives Philomena a slight smile. Philomena thinks that he looks like the shadow of his former self. Hunched up. Philomena tries to smile at this stranger. As she studies the figure opposite, he could be anybody and in a way she guesses he is. Prison has changed him. She remembers that they had always got on well. She had taken their bond for granted, and thought it unbreakable. But now, it seems this man before her is a total stranger. She wants to tell her brother that she loves him, tell him that his life still has meaning. The face that fails to meet her eye, is different. It seems this new person's ears are closed and his mind has put up barriers. Presumably, no matter what she says now, it might only push him further away.

She asks in a hollow voice, "how are you ?" She wishes him well, but she knows her voice is stumbling for the right words. It seems that Patrick is in transition to becoming a person Philomena knows he would never want to be.

Finally, however, he speaks. "All right I suppose, given my circumstances." The bitterness in his voice rises like bile into his mouth. Finally he manages, "sorry sis. Thanks for coming."

He holds his hand outstretched and Philomena places her own hand on top of his. She glances round at the prison guard across the room. There are other visitors as well. She decides to speak quietly and slowly. "Listen, I can't say too much, but there might be a chance of nailing your boss Lincoln. Remember Anna, my flatmate ? " she whispers, "she's in the police."

Patrick's expression doesn't change. He stays silent.

Philomena continues. "She leans forward confidentially, "Your friend, 'Greg', wants to come in and see you." She winks. "Would that be OK ?"

Patrick looks up and meets her eye. "I'm not saying anything," he says quietly and deliberately.

Philomena stares at him and mouths, "please !"

Patrick shrugs his shoulders.

Philomena pushes her hand across the table. Patrick reluctantly responds. Philomena squeezes his outstretched hand and smiles. "Chin up." She smiles again and then gets up to leave. She doesn't look back.

---

(19) Who Murdered Tom Preston ?

"There's no limit to how complicated things can get, on account of one thing always leading to another."
(E.B. White)

Back at the station after visiting Fred Preston's place of work and found he has not appeared there in recent days, Anna and Roger report back to DI Frank Fernbank.

"Well. How did you get on with our Mr Preston ?" asks Frank.

Anna explains the situation. "I can't put my finger on it but I'm sure that Preston knows more than he is telling us."

Roger nods agreement.

"M'mm," says Frank. "Do you think he knows, or has an idea of why young Tom was killed and in such a bizzare manner ?"

Anna and Roger exchange glances. Roger speaks first. "I did wonder whether Preston has been up to no good. For instance, if he's been involved in criminal activity himself, could the murder of his son be a very nasty way of warning him not to do something to draw attention to them or even speaking to us."

"M'mm," Frank muses. Despite us taking the Lydon gang off the streets, it's opened up a gap which I'm sure some very unpleasant characters are only too pleased to fill."

Anna and Roger nod their agreement.

Roger says," if Preston was part of a gang, it could explain why he's being so difficult to question. We know that psychologically gangs steal independence from people involved with them, a piece at a time. Over time they push the guy slightly further. In time, he loses his moral code. He begins to think that their way of thinking is the right one. In Preston's case, his son, a law-abiding citizen, becomes his enemy. He can control his wife, but not Tom. Then one day, he does something which endangers the safety of his son. Maybe Tom found out what his dad was up to and threatened to give him up to us. Maybe Preston only realised the serious problem he had created when he discovers, too late, that his own actions have directly contributed to his son's murder. Maybe in a moment of deep remorse, he's done a vanishing act. Maybe he fears he'll be next on the death list."

Frank looks impressed. "Blimey, Roger, that course you attended on the psychology of the criminal might have paid off!"

Anna nods her agreement. Roger grins.

Frank adds, "So if we proceed on that possibility, it seems highly unlikely that Preston is going to go home. He needs a hideout. To decide what to do and maybe, think of a way of punishing the criminals he's been working with."

Anna chips in. "I agree. It's unlikely for him to go home. If we're right, that would put his wife, as well as him, in danger."

They all take a pause to think through what might have happened.

Roger adds, "what if young Tom had discovered what his dad was up to ?"

Frank considers for a moment and then instructs, "Anna, I want you to speak to Mrs Preston again. Just try and see if there's any indication of suspicion on her part about her husband's goings-on. Be gentle but firm....well I don't need to tell you that. Did she have the slightest idea what hubby may have been up to ? "

Anna nods.

Frank then speaks to Roger. "Go back to Preston's place of work. Speak to his colleagues. Without suggesting any of our suspicions, see if anyone takes the bait."

Roger agrees.

Frank adds, "I'm going to interview Tony Blake and see what emerges. With any luck, we might find a link between Preston senior and Tony Blake. Could be drugs. Could be something else. We have to find out whether there's a link or not."

Frank goes to the interview room to speak with Tony Blake. He has left him in the cells for several hours. He hopes this might help to loosen his tongue. He also had to wait for a colleague, DS Jones, from the Drug Squad to join him. It might intimidate Blake more to have both officers interviewing him. Tony is brought into the interview room by PC Walker. He's clearly nervous, but tries to act tough.

PC Walker is instructed to sit on a chair by the door for the duration of the interview.

The two interviewing officers introduce themselves. Frank notices that Blake is becoming increasingly nervous.

Two experienced interviewing officers know well that a good investigator should focus on asking short, to-the-point, questions such as "Who told you that?" and "What did she say to you?" and "Where were you during this conversation?" and "How did that make you feel?" and "What happened next ?

"Frank begins. "Anthony Blake, you have been brought here in respect of your involvement in drug-taking and drug dealing. It also seems possible that you were involved in the murder of Thomas Preston, known to you as a work colleague.What do you have to say ?"

Blake's eyes widen and he looks genuinely puzzled. "Tom ? Come on, he's a mate !."

"Haven't you read the papers or seen the news on television ?"

Blake shakes his head. Frank registers that he looks genuinely shocked at the news. There's a long pause and the two interviewing officers know that keeping mum at such a time could yield results.

Tony Blake spends time grappling with his conscience. Then he speaks. "Look you've got me bang to rights on the drug front. That said, I'm only a very small cog in a big machine." He stops and looks down as if studying something on the floor. "I don't want to be connected to Tom's murder. That's barmy."

"Well, you spill the beans on the drug front," suggests DS Jones, "and we'll see what we can do on the murder front."

Blake wriggles uncomfortably on his chair. He remains silent. He has a sullen look on his face.

Frank Fernbank waits a few minutes and then says sharply. "Look mate, you are in big trouble. The longer you prevaricate, the worse it's going to be for you because we shall assume the worst…..Got that ? "

"I wasn't involved in no murder. Honest. Reg Houghton is the one who got me involved in the drugs racket. When I started to work for him, he kept hinting that he had a job on the side for me…… I didn't want to get involved. After all, I haven't got a record with you lot."

Frank nods. "That could just mean you've been very clever, son."

"He kept on until I gave in. He said it was small scale…the drugs racket. Just 'recreational' stuff you know. Cannabis, not heroin or cocaine, nor nothing like that."

"You know, however, that growing or dealing in cannabis or amphetamines is illegal don't you ?"

Blake nods reluctantly.

"Tell us more about Reg Houghton," says DS Jones.

"Well, at the start I thought he was telling the truth. You know, not weighty stuff. Then once I got started, things changed. He started getting heavy. A couple of the men he worked for came to the garage one day. Nasty looking pair. One, I don't know his name, threatened me. 'Guess you're attached to your fingernails,' he says. I knew then that I was in much deeper than I realised."

"You say you can't name either of these men. Give me a description of the one who threatened you."

Blake hesitates. He's clearly frightened. "I dunno," he says nervously.

"Look son," says Frank Fernbank, " if what you tell us reveals the identity of these men, that will go in your favour when the case goes to court."

Blake sighs. "The one who threatened me was older. Maybe in his thirties. Black hair, slicked back in a Teddy Boy style. Wearing an expensive looking suit.......the other bloke was younger, muscular. Looked like he'd done a bit of boxing.They were, well, intimidating to say the least. "

"And what did Reg Houghton do while this was going on ?" Frank makes eye contact with Blake, increasing his nervousness.

"He kept out of the way."

"M'mm, says Frank. "How come Tom got tied up in this ?"

Blake hesitates. "I'm not sure, but I reckon Reg might have put him under pressure. See, one day, the older bloke comes in and he and Reg are in the office rattling on nineteen to the dozen. There's a bit of a fracas and Tom says to me that he's going in to see what it's all about. Well I had to stop him. Told him it was a dissatisfied customer and Reg was quite capable of sorting it out."

"Was Tom suspicious ?" asks DS Jones.

"He wouldn't have known nothing about the drug business, but I reckon he was suspicious about the argument. You could hear the pair of them shouting from outside the garage. When the bloke left, he drives off in a fancy Jag. Tom says he couldn't remember that Jag coming in the garage for repairs or a service. It weren't one we sold neither."

"So Tom thought there was something going on ? Did he discuss it with you ?" Frank Fernbank watches closely to see Blake's response.

"No. He might have thought that I didn't know nothing about the argument. He was suspicious like. Something struck him as dodgy, but he couldn't put his finger on it."

"Right. We'll leave things there at the moment," instructs Frank. "You will return to the cells and consider your position. You will be charged on the drugs front. Any involvement in Thomes Preston's death will mean a murder charge."

Blake looks very scared. "Honest to God guv, I didn't know nothin' about that.I liked young Tom. Wouldn't have wanted to see him getting tied up in drugs. No, Reg Houghton's your man, I swear."

Frank tells PC Walker to take Blake back to the cells.

"What d'you reckon ?" asks Frank.

DS Jones replies, "On the drugs front, he seems a bit too naive. I reckon he knows more than he's letting on. After all, your officers found the remains of cannabis 'joints', so he's not as innocent as he's trying to make out. That said, I believe him on the murder front. It doesn't fit."

Frank nods. "I'm inclined to agree. If he's telling the truth, looks like we need to bring Reg Houghton in for questioning pronto."

"Agreed. Let's hope your team can get their hands on Fred Preston as well."

DS Jones leaves the room, leaving Frank Fernback to mull over the emerging situation.

---

(20) Unravelling the Fraud

"People are getting more creative and sophisticated in their fraud schemes." (Devorah Goldburg)

Anna and Roger and the rest of the team have been called into the station for a discussion with a Detective Inspector Parkin from the Met's Fraud squad. He is going to explain the necessary steps for initiating a formal fraud investigation in respect of John Lincoln.

DI Jack Parkin is a man in middle-age. He has dark brown hair which is greying at the sides and he wears glasses which give him a kind of academic appearance.

Frank Fernbank introduces him to the assembled group and explains the subject for this session, which is to form an essential start to the managing of the fraud investigation in which Roger and Anna will be involved.

DI Parkin has prepared some typed notes which he hands out to those present.

"I hope this will be useful to you," he begins in an authoritative voice. "To complete a fraud investigation, you must follow five key steps. These are recorded for you in the notes. The first step is to perform an initial evaluation. This is where you are starting. I understand from your boss – he looks at Frank – I understand two members of your team are carrying out some key initial work in this respect. He points to Roger and Anna. Remember that this is only the preliminary stage. Once you have more material to work with...and I understand that you are making progress in this respect, you can then move on to step two which is to make an investigation plan. DI Fernbank here will designate tasks as appropriate. Then comes the practical work, speaking to key people involved in the matter and keeping tight notes on what you discover. Then comes step three. Together with your boss you will review and analyse the data you have collected. The more the better because step four is to conduct interviews with anyone you have decided could be, or is, involved in some way. Then prepare a report. If necessary you may need to widen your search for both people and information. I understand that some homeless people are involved and, of course, it's difficult to pin down itinerant bods.

These steps should typically unfold as follows. It will be DI Fernbank's job as the main Fraud Investigator in this case, to ensure that these steps are followed and completed to the best of your ability. Think of these steps as a tool kit which will help in understanding the situation and the scenario. Remember, obtain any relevant documents you can and perform background checks on any suspects. Use surveillance where needed, use informants to carry out any undercover operations deemed necessary." He looks at Roger. " I understand you are to visit a prisoner who may possibly be innocent in this case ?"

"Yes," agrees Roger.

"I don't have to tell you about conducting interviews and interrogation tactics. Maybe any physical evidence can be laboratory analysed. We are going to be on hand when necessary. We will become involved at a later date to go through what has been happening. Remember, fraud offences are recognised as being one of the most frequently reported and complex crimes for us to investigate. OK, well that's me done. He looks at each of the team. Good luck with this. It sounds a bit of a stinker, but I'm sure you'll get to the bottom of it."

Detective Inspector Parkin collects his papers and leaves the room.

Frank Fernbank addresses the team. "Right, you'll work in pairs. You'll need to get to know the regulars at the hostel and speak to them as well as any staff and volunteers. If you pick up on anything and I mean anything, report back and we'll arrange further action. Keep tight notes. DI Edwards and DS Kinsale will allocate the tasks……Dismissed."

The members of the team leave the room.

Roger and Anna have remained behind. Frank addresses Roger. . "Well now, this'll be an experience for you ! Still, all grist to the mill…. Roger, you're visiting Patrick O'Farrell tomorrow ?"

"That's right guv."

"Go easy on him. He may well be in a fragile state. First time in prison is tough, especially for an educated bloke like him. See what you think. If you reckon he could be in danger, the prison authorities need to know so they can keep an eye on him."

"Will do."

Frank turns to Anna. "I want you to have words with your flatmate. As the sister of O'Farrell, she can tell you about his personality. How's he going to manage in the nick ?"

Anna replies. "She visited her brother yesterday. I was wary of bringing up a conversation about how it went, but I could see she was in a bit of a state. She's worried about him. Mentally and physically."

" I can believe that," says Frank. He looks at Roger. "Be very careful about how you speak to him."

Anna chips in. "I think she hinted to him that he might get a visit from a 'friend'. Not sure how that went in though or what his reaction will be."

"Slowly, slowly catchee monkey," adds Frank.

(21) Who Dunnit ?

"The truth must be quite plain, if one could just clear away the litter."
(Agatha Christie, A Caribbean Mystery)

Anna calls at the home of Fred and Elsie Preston. Elsie answers the doorbell. She looks exhausted. Anna notices that Elsie seems to be working herself up into a state of panic. She hesitates before inviting Anna in. Anna knows she has to tread carefully.

"Would you like a cup of tea ? Elsie asks politely.

"That would be lovely. Thank you. Anna smiles and follows Elsie into the kitchen. She sits at the kitchen table while Elsie busies herself making the tea.

Anna decides to pitch in. "I understand your husband has taken time off work. I do understand it must be an awful time for you both."

Elsie doesn't reply.

"He's out at the moment is he ?" asks Anna, adding "I expect he needs a bit of fresh air from time to time ?"

Elsie doesn't reply. She places the cups and saucers, milk jug and sugar bowl on a tray and heads for the sitting room. Anna follows and offers to pour the tea.

"Thank you, dear," says Elsie.

There's a silence whilst they both take a sip of tea and then replace their cups and saucers back on the tray. Elsie looks down at her lap, avoiding Anna's eye.

"Mrs Preston….Elsie…." begins Anna gently. "I'm sorry to upset you, but as I'm sure you understand, we must find Tom's killer."

Elsie continues to look down. She nods, but doesn't speak.

"Will Fred be back soon ?" Anna asks, deliberately using Mr Preston's first name to keep things in a gentle and familiar style.

"He spends a lot of time out of the house. I think……." she hesitates, "he's trying to do his own investigation. He has to feel he's doing something or he'll go mad."

Anna smiles sympathetically. "Do you know what he's been doing ? Has he found anything out ?"

Elsie looks awkward. "He's got the idea……….welll……Oh dear. I'll tell you anyway. You see he's knows you're investigating things, but he's got it into his head that somehow Reg Houghton is involved." She looks at Anna.

"Really ? What makes him think that ?"

Elsie looks at Anna awkwardly. "I think Fred might be hiding stuff from me. You know, so as not to upset me. He's got it in his head that Reg and also, maybe, that Tony fella, might be up to no good. Criminals you know. Nicking stuff. Burglaries. He reckons that Tony is a wrong 'un."

Anna's ears prick up. "What makes him think that ?"

"Well apparently, some very iffy looking characters have been hanging about the garage when Fred was visiting. Tom had already told him about it. Said him and Tony saw a very iffy pair coming to see Reg. There was a lot of shouting. Tom said Tony told him it was a bloke who wasn't happy with repairs Reg had done to his car. The car was a Jag. Tom said to Tony that they hadn't sold a Jag recently and certainly hadn't done a service on one. Tony just shrugged his shoulders.Wouldn't say no more. That made Fred think there was something dodgy going on there. if Tony and Reg were up to something together he was convinced that might have been a reason to kill our Tom. We both thought maybe Tom had said he was going to tell the police and that's why they………" Tears fill Elsie's eyes and run down her cheeks."

Anna takes her hand. "I understand. I promise I'll tell my boss, DI Fernbank. It gives us something to be going on with. Look, I appreciate that Fred wants to do something rather than sitting at home moping. Reassure him we are working on the case. If he tells us what he's discovered, then that gives us more to go on. makes it more likely to catch the right culprit or culprits."

Elsie gives her a watery smile. "I know you'll do your best, dear. Fred's so worked up you see because he thought that he and Reg were friends. All this has really upset the apple cart."

Anna finishes her tea and Elsie shows her to the door. Anna lays her hand on Elsie's arm. "Don't worry, we'll get to the bottom of this. I promise……Listen, tell Fred that any information he gets, he should share with us. It's all grist to the mill."

Elsie nods. Anna makes her way back to her car. She knows now they have to speak to Fred Preston urgently. Seems he's not a baddie, she tells herself.

(22) Murray Gets Involved

Helping others is like helping yourself.
(Henry Flagler)

Frank Fernbank has organised a visit by himself and Anna to Stratford Police Station. Anna has, with Frank's approval, already spoken to Murray about the case. Murray is waiting for them in his office with a thick file of paperwork on his desk.

Murray smiles at Anna who finds herself blushing for some unknown reason and she chides herself and tells herself to be professional in this situation.

Murray gives Anna a brief smile and then turns to DCI Fernbank. "So Frank, let's hear your thoughts on this case."

Frank acknowledges that the information he has already was given by Anna and is based on what she has gleaned from her flatmate, Philomena, O'Farrell's sister.

"M'mm" says Murray, opening the file. "I've had a look through the case notes. DCI Ted Merriman was in charge of the case. Course, he's retired now, that's why I'm here. I'm going to try and speak to Ted, see what he can recall from the start. Anyhow, from what I've gleaned from the case notes, it seems now that John Lincoln, the Manager of Help the Homeless, has been a very clever character. On all the occasions he was interviewed, he seemed the genuine article. He was sad about what had happened. Sorry that he had employed Patrick O'Farrell, believing him to be honest and dedicated to helping the homeless. If it was all an act, he's certainly been a clever bugger."

Murray looks up from the paperwork and speaks to Frank and Anna. " Now I am thinking that he may well have conned the lot of us. Playing the innocent and having account books that seemed to all intents and purposes genuine, at least on the surface."

Frank nods. "The trustees are going to look into the matter. They need to check the accounts back from when Lincoln began as Manager. It's five years' worth, so it could take a while !"

Murray hands the case notes to Frank Fernbank. "Have a read of this lot to familiarise you with the details of the case. If DI Edwards is going to visit O'Farrell, a read of this lot and a chat with me after I've spoken to Ted Merriman should be of help."

Frank takes the file and thanks Murray.

Murray stands up, leaving his desk to open the door for them both. He shakes Frank's hand and smiles at Anna. "See you later," he whispers in her ear.

Anna feels her cheeks reddening.

---

(23) Roger's Prison Visit

"Once you choose hope, anything is possible." (unknown)

After their training session in respect of fraud and following the meeting with Murray and discussion of the file, Frank Fernbank calls Roger into his office to plan for his meeting in prison with Patrick O'Farrell the following day.

"It's important to cultivate a relationship with O'Farrell. Don't expect to get every bit of information on the first visit. You may have to spend time establishing and then maintaining a more personal relationship with him. Essentially, you're covertly using the relationship you build up, to obtain information or to provide access to any information about the others possibly involved in this dodgy affair."

Roger nods his head. "I've had a bit of undercover experience over the years with informants and witnesses, but that was just me and them. It's more complex this time because I'm treading on thin ice if what his sister has said to Anna is true. The bloke's in a fragile state and he could just clam up."

Frank nods. "You can only do your best. Chances are it may need more than one visit."

Roger nods agreement. The following day begins with a tremendous thunderstorm. It brings with it electric skies and rain that shouts on the rooftops and drums against every surface around. DI Roger Edwards has left his car at the station and borrowed what he calls 'an old banger' to drive to his prison appointment. He's dressed in scruffy blue jeans and a T-shirt which boasts a print of The Rolling Stones. He smiles as he thinks that the logo 'Paint it Black' a newly released number, fits well with the weather.

It's quite a short drive to the prison, although there's the inevitable and continuous traffic jam through the streets of the city.

Once he arrives he parks in the allocated spaces in front of the building. The building is formidable. Built in Victorian times, it looks both gloomy and dispiriting. How would a man like Patrick O'Farrell feel when he was grasped in the cruel arms of such a desolate place ?

Roger knows that he is now in character, like an actor. The prison governor had approved his visit, but the other prison staff are not aware of his real identity. He is stopped at the first barrier where he explains his name is Johnny Skipton and he is visiting a friend, Patrick O'Farrell. He is searched for any hidden weapons or drugs and then allowed through to another area where a prison warder directs him to what is the visitors' room. Several prisoners and their visitors are already engaged in conversation. The warder who has shown him into the room catches the eye of a younger warder by clicking his fingers. The second man disappears through a door and shortly afterwards returns with Patrick O'Farrell. The prisoner is shown to an upright wooden chair placed at a small table. Roger is seated opposite him.

Patrick looks nervous. Roger speaks loudly with a view to informing both Patrick and the warders present of his name. "Well now, Pat, I bet you weren't expecting a visit from your old mate, Johnny ?"

"No," replies Patrick nervously. He doesn't make eye contact with Roger.

"Thought I'd better call in and see my old buddy. I heard from your sister that you were in nick. I never knew....How long have you been here ?"

"Three months now," replies Patrick quietly, not making eye contact and looking down at the surface of the table as if something fascinating could be found there.

"Yeah well I thought it was about time I visited you."

Patrick shrugs his shoulders and continues to look down.

"How's it going ?" asks Roger gently, hoping to elicit a response by speaking in a gentle, calm manner.

Patrick remains silent.

This time, Roger leans over the table willing Patrick to look up. He speaks quietly. "Listen mate, the coppers have had some information about your case. Remember, your mate Danny ?"

At the sound of this name Patrick looks up and briefly makes eye contact. He nods warily.

Roger whispers. "Well, between Danny and your sister, they've got the authorities interested in your case again."

Patrick turns his head slightly to the right. Roger looks in the same direction. He sees that the warder in charge of the visitors' area is walking around and heading in their direction. Roger changes tack. "You'd laugh mate. Remember Barney Slater ?"

Patrick cottons on and plays ball. "Yeah. What about him ?"

"You know his penchant for the ladies. Well, can you believe, his old woman has been making him stay at home ! s'pect he's been a naughty boy once too often !"

Patrick manages a watery smile.

The warder strolls past them without making any comment or even looking in their direction.

Roger continues the banter for a while and Patrick does finally try to laugh. Eventually, Roger looks at his watch. "Better make my way, mate. I'll pop in again." He winks at Patrick. Chin up fella."

"Thanks," says Patrick quietly.

Roger feels disappointed with himself for how little information he had gained. Maybe he could arrange a second visit and get Patrick to open up more. He will report back and decide how he should move forward.

---

(24) Fraud at 'Help the Homeless'

"Nothing matters but the facts. Without them, the science of criminal investigation is nothing more than a guessing game."
(Blake Edwards)

Anna is in her office at the police station. Both Frank Fernbank and Roger Edwards are elsewhere. She's looking through the file on Patrick O'Farrell to familiarise herself with the facts of the case. His arrest and imprisonment seem to have happened quite quickly. John Lincoln, the manager of the Help the Homeless hostel, had explained how Patrick could have stolen the money from the hostel. Essentially, because he was often working alone and was responsible for paying money into the bank. It seems that the officers working on the case had believed John Lincoln and accepted his explanation of how Patrick O'Farrell could have stolen the money. Lincoln seemed to have played the part of the disappointed boss. He'd trusted Patrick, he'd said, naively believing him to be an honest and trustworthy employee. Anna surmises that Lincoln had been so convincing that, maybe, it resulted in the investigating team ignoring any denials by Patrick. He had been a new employee. Money thefts had coincided with his appointment to the post. It seemed cut and dried. Now, in retrospect, suspicions are being raised. If Patrick is innocent, then maybe John Lincoln was the thief. Anna decides that another visit to the hostel is needed. If she and Roger speak to Lincoln maybe something might emerge to help throw light on a different scenario.

Anna decides to take the bull by the horns and make an appointment to visit the hostel and speak to John Lincoln again. She finds the telephone number and rings it. A female voice answers.

"My name is Detective Sergeant Anna Kinsale. I wondered if it would be possible to speak with Mr John Lincoln please ?"

"I'm afraid he's not here at the moment. Can I help ?"

"I would really like to speak to Mr Lincoln. When are you expecting him back? "

"I'm afraid he's on leave at present."

"Oh, I see. When are you expecting him back ?"

There's a pause, then the voice says, "we're not sure. He's taking indefinite leave. Personal reasons I understand."

The air is so brittle it might crack. Warning bells sound in Anna's ears.

There's a long pause, but Anna can hear breathing on the other end of the phone.

As Anna considers what to say next, the female voice returns to the line. "I wonder," the voice says nervously, "if I could speak to you in confidence."

"Of course. Can I take your name ?"

" Janet Gardner." She hesitates. " Since Mr Lincoln has been away, I am beginning to have more concerns about him. It's not just me. There are a number of regular customers at the hostel who don't trust him. I've been having suspicions about the way donations are being used."

Anna tells Janet that she would like to speak to her away from the hostel. Janet gives Anna her address and says that she will be at home this evening after 6pm.

Anna is impatient to speak further with Janet. Maybe this could reveal something which might help Patrick. She remains in the office and leaves later, taking her own car to the address she has been given. She arrives at a Victorian house which has been converted into flats. Looking at the names on the doorbells she finds the relevant button. It's early evening and Janet will now be home. She presses the button. Shortly afterwards, a dark-haired woman of about Anna's own age opens the front door. She is dressed in what might be termed 'hippy' clothes. A flowery, flowing skirt and a t-shirt decorated with a picture of the Rolling Stones.

Anna holds up her ID and introduces herself. She is invited in and follows Janet to the first floor. Inside, the flat is similar to her own. Anna notices that Janet has modernised the decor and created a light and comfortable home. Janet directs Anna to an armchair and offers her tea.

Shortly afterwards, she returns with a tray. Pouring the tea, she speaks to Anna. She seems uncomfortable. "I must say I have had my own suspicions ever since Patrick was arrested, but it seemed such an open and closed case as far as the police were concerned.....sorry...."

Anna smiles. "No, please go on."

Well," begins Janet, "I trained as an accountant. I've always had the idea that I'd like to work for a charity, so when this offer of a job arose, I thought I'd take it. I left my job in the City and decided to get some first-hand experience of working for a charity, so that, maybe, at a later date I could get a better paid job in that field. I know salaries have to be low, but I've always had a desire to take my career in that direction."

"What were you doing in the City ?" asks Anna.

"I worked for a large bank. Well paid, but a bit...well...boring." She grins at Anna.

Anna smiles.

"When I was offered the role of helper, well, general dogsbody, at 'Help the Homeless', I was thrilled. It was my dream job, but now I am tempted to resign. I feel so disillusioned. I don't think I did enough to help your original investigation, but I had no proof. On the other hand, I feel now that I ought to stay and try and get some proof of the theft of funds....." She pauses, looking Anna in the eye. "I knew I couldn't contact the police without being able to offer some proof."

"I understand," agrees Anna.

Janet continues. "A few weeks into the job I started to notice that something wasn't right. Patrick had been involved in banking the monies received, but when I got sight of the books, the income and expenditure figures didn't seem to match the budget that had been agreed with the trustees. Despite, by my estimate, good income from donations, the accounts showed the charity to be in the red. I felt I couldn't do anything about it until I'd spent some time working there."

She pauses and takes a sip of tea. "I soon noticed that Mr Lincoln had begun to make drastic proposals to the trustees, suggesting that reserves should be used to slash costs. It was a difficult and worrying time for me and everyone involved. Most are really dedicated, but Mr Lincoln was consistently reassuring us about how the finances were dealt with. When the trustees asked for cash flow figures he produced them, confidently assuring them all was well. He boasted that they were not to worry and he would take sole care of all the incomings and outgoings. I felt so frustrated and helpless. Even if I'd reported it to the trustees, I was a new employee and Mr Lincoln has been in situ for around five years."

Anna nods. " I see the problem. The trouble is, like you, we need some proof of wrongdoing before we can act." She thinks and an idea comes to her. "Could you give me a list of the trustees ? Maybe one of them might personally know someone in the police force, someone high ranking. Just a quiet, informal tip-off might open a can of worms."

Janet perks up and smiles. "A good idea. I can do that for you tomorrow morning and provide all their contact details."

The two women finish their tea and smile at one another. Both are relieved that a storm may be approaching for John Lincoln and any of his accomplices. Anna bids Janet farewell. She can't wait to report back to her boss and the team.

---

(25) Onward & Upward

"spilling the beans"

Much as she would have liked to tell Philomena about the prison visit by Roger to see her brother, Anna knows this is confidential and strictly police business, so she can't say anything to endanger further prison visits by Roger.

Roger has reported back the results of his visit. He had managed to tell Patrick O'Farrell that the case was now being reconsidered. He explains how Patrick seems depressed and deeply unhappy. He hopes that his visit and what he had told him will have some positive effect.

"Well you've set the scene," Frank Fernbank assures him. "It may involve patience and several visits by you to elicit some answers and find out about O'Farrell's knowledge or theories about exactly what had been happening before he got the blame."

Roger nods agreement.

Frank continues. "Our aim is to wheedle out as much information as possible from O'Farrell. However, you mustn't step over an imaginary line which could elicit some information, some names, but at the expense of O'Farrell's safety in prison."

Roger remembers a course he had attended on how to use informants. He had used the advice with a number of informants over his recent career. Many of these strategies could also be applied in dealing with a situation like that of Patrick O'Farrell. Roger had learned that many of the points made and advice given at that time was to relate to and appreciate the moral significance and power dynamics at play in such a relationship. He was very aware of such issues. His knowledge and experience as a police officer meant that dealing with such relationships embodies great moral and emotional tension, both for the police officer and the informant. O'Farrell was in a delicate position and a mistake by Roger could lead to who knows what revenge might be taken if word got back to those implicated in the fraud.

All police officers were taught that using informants was regarded as an important and necessary police tactic for gaining intelligence on a variety of criminal activities and those involved. However, a new generation of senior ranks had the feeling that some of the work done could be regarded as 'dirty work'. It was not unusual for informants to be pressurised hard into giving information that they were reluctant to impart. The potential for the police-informant relationship was valuable when investigating crimes, but sometimes littered with morally troubling and highly emotive activities. Informants had traditionally been a stigmatised group thought to be worthy of contempt. Roger knew that Frank Fernbank, who was an excellent DCI, was what might be termed 'old school'. Roger and no doubt Anna, as she progressed in her job, were more aware of the morality issues in the relationship between police officers and their informants being taken seriously.

On his visit to see him, Roger had been made aware of the fragility and vulnerability of Patrick O'Farrell and he knew that Anna felt the same. In fact, Anna, being close to O'Farrell's sister and the contacts she had come across in her investigations so far, knew how emotional and vulnerable both Philomena and her brother were. Roger determined that the power dynamics at play within this situation required very careful handling.

Most recently, the role of informants had gradually begun changing. Threats or even police brutality and coercion were becoming increasingly frowned upon. Both Roger and Anna had attended a course which had emphasised the importance of seeking to obtain alternative forms of collecting insights and evidence. Covert methods, such as Roger's visit to Patrick O'Farrell posing as a friend, were slowly being recognised as ways of eliminating police corruption. The relationship between detectives and other criminals or witnesses was influencing the direction of reforms. Together, these developments were gradually resulting in a conscious effort to make the police force more 'professional'. Changes were seeing the implementation of bureaucratic systems of registration and monitoring within police forces, and a greater demarcation between informants and their 'handlers' – the latter being those police officers responsible for the day-to-day management of their informants. Other senior officers were known as 'controllers' These officers had general oversight and responsibility for ensuring the relationship between the handler and informant was carefully monitored. Unfortunately there were those older police officers for whom the 'professionalisation' agenda was met with cultural resistance. In such instances, a continued use of unregistered informants and a reluctance to follow administrative procedures emerged. On occasion, these different perspectives resulted in clashes between the officers concerned in a particular case.

---

(26) Death and Deception

"Oh, what a tangled web we weave...when first we practice to deceive."
(Walter Scott, Marmion)

Anna and Roger have been given the task of speaking to Reg Houghton again. Bearing in mind what they now know about him from the information revealed by Tony Blake, they need to go in hard. Did his wife know anything ? Is he linked to Tom Preston's death ?

They arrive at the garage to find the main vehicle entrance doors are locked. However, a smaller pedestrian gate at the side is open. The pair enter cautiously. The garage is empty. No sign of Reg Houghton. That said, in the small makeshift office, the light is on and a woman they recognise as Mrs Houghton is busy on the typewriter. Roger knocks on the door and makes her jump.

"Oh sorry," says Mrs Houghton, "I wasn't expecting anyone today." She looks at both of them. "He's not here you see. Reg, I mean. He's off on business. Gone to look at a car he might be interested in acquiring......"

Roger nods, but doesn't speak. He's hoping Mrs Houghton might reveal something useful. People often like to fill in a blank space in a conversation.

The woman looks embarrassed. "I don't know when he'll be back. He'll probably come here first, but......."

"Don't worry," reassures Anna. "Where is it he's gone ?"

She flicks through an untidy pile of paper. "Doesn't say."

"Does your husband often leave the garage for any length of time ?" asks Roger.

"Well, you see dear, he leaves Tony….and of course, poor Tom before…..well you know…..in charge of the mechanical side of repairs and servicing. Reg deals with the customers and the car sales. Mind you, trade's a bit slow at the moment I'm afraid. It's why he's having to travel further afield for vehicles, you know."

Anna and Roger exchange glances. So, thinks Anna, he could be up to anything while he's away.

"So no-one is here to deal with customers apart from yourself ?" asks Roger.

"That's right dear. I always take a message. Trouble is Tony's still off sick and what with ……..well you know, Tom………things are a bit difficult."

"Have you heard from Tony ?" asks Anna, knowing that he's safely in police custody.

"No dear. It's suprising really because I said to Reg that I'd try and phone Tony and find out when he was coming back. Reg was a bit sharp with me and told me not to contact him under any circumstances." She shrugged her shoulders. "Well, he's the boss, but I tell you he's going to lose custom if this goes on."

"Well, thank you Mrs Houghton," says Roger. "Please contact either myself or Sergeant Kinsale here, when your husband returns. We do need to speak to him as soon as possible."

Mrs Houghton looks a little confused. "If you say so dear."

The two police officers return to their car.

"The plot thickens." states Roger.

Anna is driving and they make their way back to the police station.

Once back in the office, Anna finds a telephone directory listing numbers in the Chelmsford area. No garage or car dealers are listed in the name of Johnson. 'M'mm, strange,' thinks Anna. 'So where are you Reg Houghton ?' She asks the question aloud.

"Talking to yourself now are we ?", asks the voice of Frank Fernbank, as he enters the room.

Anna explains the mystery.

Roger has been to the canteen and returns with three coffees.

"Right," says Frank firmly. "So where are you, Mr Reg Houghton ?" He considers for a moment. "I think we need to find and speak to chummy, pronto." He considers. "OK, Anna, you keep phoning Houghton's garage. If he's not returned, you and Roger go to his home and see if he's appeared there. Check with Mrs Houghton. Push her a bit. Maybe she knows more than she's saying. We don't want him doing a runner if he's up to no good. While you're on the phone, try ringing Elsie Preston again. Tell her that her husband must call into the police station pronto."

Frank finishes his coffee and returns upstairs.

Anna tries ringing the Preston's home number and Roger tries both the Houghton's home and garage numbers. No response from either. So, neither man has returned. Anna and Roger discuss the case as it is so far. Could they have missed something ? Had they missed any clues ? Nothing jumps out at them.

"Ok," says Roger, you focus on Fred Preston. I'll go with Reg Houghton. We'll keep in touch over the radio, but if it's no go, make your way back here. I'll go via the garage and if Houghton's not there, I'll go to his house. I think we'll have to put some pressure on the wives. Are they completely unaware of what their other halves are up to ? Or, are they keeping schtum ?"

---

(27) Where is Philomena ?

"Nothing good ever comes of violence."

(Martin Luther)

August 1967

Anna arrives home, makes a quick cup of tea and throws herself down on the sofa. She's been waiting and searching for Fred Preston but he seems to have disappeared off the face of the earth ! Roger's had no luck with tracking down Reg Houghton. Each of them has obtained a photograph of the man being searched for. If neither man returns home overnight, Frank Fernbank plans to release the pictures to the newspapers, television and radio news. They will keep looking in the meantime. Uniformed officers have been posted for an all night surveillance on both the homes and places of work of the two men.

Despite Anna's exhaustion, she knows that even when she is tired her brain keeps on going as if it were in some Olympic race. She tries to relax and sips her tea. The feeling of being a runner begins to subside. Her brain is soon running on only five percent battery. She wants to consider the case and how far things have got and what will come next. Firstly though, she decides she needs to take time out. After her rest she will soak in the calm peace of a warm bath. This case, this caring, is vast, yet finally may prove to be finite. She yawns and feels tired... so very, very, tired.

Later, having had a bath and changed into a towelling dressing gown, Anna returns to the sofa and puts her feet up. She looks at the clock. Philomena told her this morning that she'd be back around five o'clock. She'd been on early shift at the hospital so would be finished at about two o'clock. She was then going for a swim after work with another nurse, a friend named Jane Baker. It was seven now and no sign. Still, she must have got delayed.

Anna lies back and goes over the details of both the Patrick O'Farrell case and the murder of Tom Preston. Each is beginning to seem like closed doors, temptingly unlocked, but that won't open. Anna closes her eyes and pushes at each door handle, but although they move, the doors appear to be locked from the inside and access seems impossible.

There's no way she can even squeeze through either. The doors stay firmly shut. Take a step back, she tells herself. Start at the beginning. She gives each door one final stare as if her frustration could open it and then gets up in a huff whn nothing happens.

Two hours later, Philomena has not returned. She hasn't telephoned. Anna tries to brush off her concern. Anything could have happened. She shouldn't worry. After all, her flatmate is a fully grown adult and not her responsibility. She makes herself a snack of baked beans on toast, followed by a glass of white wine. Despite her desire to sit and relax, she can't.

Now it's nine o'clock. No telephone call from Philomena. Maybe she and her friend had decided to go for a meal or to the cinema. That was it.

Anna tries to concentrate on what she had learnt about Patrick from those who knew him at the hostel. They all thought he was a decent bloke, unlikely to have stolen donated money. So, if the fraud could be laid at the Manager, John Lincoln's, door, it was a question of getting the necessary proof. Anna begins to realise that if the homeless customers may suspect Lincoln, but have no proof to offer, it has to come down to the small number of staff or a volunteer, as indeed Patrick was. The staff have been interviewed and nothing untoward has come to light. It could mean the culprit is playing a clever game. None of them have police records, but Anna's boss, Frank Fernbank, has already suggested re-interviewing them, but the second time putting more pressure on each of them. The culprit might emerge or tell tales about a colleague if pushed. That step has begun.

Anna thinks about the volunteers. They would have known Patrick and those they had interviewed all were keen to insist that Patrick wasn't capable of such a crime. He cared about the homeless. Anna felt sympathy, even empathy with the homeless. Sitting in her comfortable flat, she tries to imagine walking out of what is her home and sitting out on the street in the cold. Not now even, but in winter. Imagine if her home was no longer her home, that it has been taken away, just at the click of fingers. She imagines her clothes, her belongings that could not be carried, are all gone. She tries to imagine having no access to food, nor having any right to eat or drink. She imagines a freezing night closing in. This is the reality of the homeless. Anna imagines sleeping in the cold with no bed, no walls, no door. Not the safety of familiar surroundings. She tries to imagine this lonely existence. Then, she imagines how many people don't have to actually imagine such a nightmare. They are living it right now, trying to survive it or recover from it. How can a society be civilised when all of this is only one bad turn, one wrong decision, away from it happening to anyone ? How can we say our nation is a family when this can happen to one of us ?

It makes Anna realise how lucky she has been with loving parents, a comfortable home and now, a good job. She has been focusing on the homeless people themselves and although she has no proof at this moment in time, she has a gut feeling that it's not one or more of the homeless people who have been involved. She determines to help in the gathering of all, if possible, of the volunteers. Maybe they haven't seen and spoken to them all. Maybe a guilty volunteer is involved and is now keeping a low profile out of the sight of the police.

In respect of the murder case, Anna begins to wonder whether it might be possible that Fred Preston had sussed out that Reg Houghton was somehow linked to Tom's death. If so, he'd certainly go after him. She hoped that , if that was the case, he wouldn't try and take justice into his own hands……..

She looks at the clock again. A quarter to ten. Her gut instinct kicks in. There's something wrong. She goes to the phone book and looks for Philomena's friend Jane Baker's home number. It's there. She dials the number. It's quickly answered by a female voice.

"Is that Jane Baker ?" asks Anna.

"Yes," a hesitant voice replies.

"I'm sorry to phone you so late, Jane, I'm Anna Kinsale, Philomena's flatmate. Philomena's not home yet. I wondered if you had been out together this evening ? I was expecting her home earlier. Sorry...I expect I sound like a Mother Hen !"

Jane laughs. "We had a swim after work and then we had an afternoon tea at Betty's. She left me about twenty to five as we left the shop and so she would have been home by five thirty at the latest.

Betty's was an old-fashioned tea shop in town. It served afternoon tea with a selection of mouth-watering scones and cakes. Anna had been there numerous times.

"And as far as you know she wasn't going anywhere else on her way home ?"

"Not that she mentioned," replies Jane, sounding puzzled.

"Look, I'm sorry to have worried you. Leave it with me and I'll phone you as soon as she gets back." Anna tries her best to sound reassuring.

"OK", answers Jane cautiously and she hangs up.

Anna can feel her heart rate increasing. Maybe there's been a road accident and Philomena has been involved or even been a witness. Anna decides to phone the station.

Soon she hears the familiar voice of Sergeant Jim Stokes who's obviously manning the desk. The sergeant is a tubby, friendly man only a year from retirement.

"Hi Jim, it's Anna." She hesitates briefly.

"Hello young Anna, what can I do you for ?" Sergeant Stokes says jokingly.

Anna smiles at his answer. It's true Jim Stokes is seen by many of the younger officers as a kind of father figure. He's kind and reassuring and deals calmly with people who enter the station in a flap about something, even something very serious.

"Jim, I know I sound as if I'm fussing, but my flatmate, Philomena, was due back home around teatime and she's not arrived yet. I spoke to a fellow nurse who worked the same shift with her and they had afternoon tea together. Afterwards Philomena was supposed to be on her way home. That's over four hours ago."

Jim is listening carefully. "You sure she hasn't met up with someone else, maybe a fella and gone off dancing or to the pictures ?"

"I think she'd have phoned me. We don't live in each other's pockets, but we know it's best to keep in touch, just in case.....well you know what I mean."

"Well now, there's not been any road accidents reported this evening. Nothing untoward that I know about."

"Would you keep me posted, Jim. Just in case."

"Will do."

"Bye."

Anna sits worrying. At least it appears that Philomena hasn't been involved in a road accident or some dodgy incident. She was just being silly. Nevertheless, that gut feeling stays fixed."

"She decides to watch TV. Maybe that will take her mind off things for now. She knows only too well that she can't report a grown woman missing until forty eight hours has passed. Nevertheless............

Anna remembers that tonight The Beatles were to perform live on BBC television's 'Top of the Pops', the UK's major television pop music show. There were two recorded songs "Paperback Writer" and on the record's B-side was "Rain". She had missed the show, but now it was being reported on the TV News and clips were being shown. She recalls that Philomena, a keen Beatles' fan, had wanted to get home in time to see them live on television. This increases Anna's concern.

Finally, Anna decides to get ready for bed, but to sleep on the sofa in the living room where she can get to the phone quickly if it rings. Despite her anxiety, she has fallen asleep.

Suddenly, she is awakened by a sound. It's someone entering the flat with a key. Anna reaches out and turns on a lamp which is positioned on a side table next to the sofa. As she rises from her sleep, the door is flung open and a figure pours into the room. For a moment it is unrecognisable. Then it strikes home. It's Philomena. When she first comes into Anna's view she doesn't recognise her. Her head is hung low and her gait is all wrong. She walks like a rag doll, floppy and lop-sided. As she nears her friend, Anna's heart falls right through her body and hits the floor. Philomena's face is more purple than pink. Her left eye is swollen. Anna thinks she can't be seeing anything out of it and knows she won't for a while yet. Her face bears congealed blood and her clothes are an utter mess. She catches Anna's eye and tries to say her name, but her cracked lips fail at the first syllable. She doesn't need to speak, Anna is already on her feet and rushing towards her.

Anna supports her friend and leads her to the sofa where she sits her down. She is clearly extremely uncomfortable. Goodness knows what injuries are hidden by the rags which were once clothes. Anna waits while the sorry figure of her flatmate tries to compose herself. While she gives her this time, she goes to the kitchen and returns with a glass of water. She gently lifts it to Philomena's face and urges her to swallow a little. Philomena does so and unsuccessfully tries to smile.

Anna is not sure whether she should call an ambulance or let Philomena rest for a little while. Deciding that there could be unseen internal injuries, she picks up the phone and dials 999. The reassuring voice of the operator tells her that an ambulance is on its way.

"She kneels beside the sorry figure. "I've called an ambulance. We need to get you to hospital and be checked over....I'll come with you," she adds.

Only ten minutes later, she hears the bell of the ambulance as it arrives outside. She goes down to meet them.

"OK, Miss, don't you worry, we'll take it from here." a tall, middle-aged man says reassuringly.

The two ambulance crew proceed into the flat where they are met with the sight of Philomena. They gently and carefully get her lying on the stretcher.

"Want to come with her ?" asks one of the ambulance crew.

"Yes," I do," says Anna quickly. No point in involving her colleagues until she can get the full story from Philomena.

Anna sits close to Philomena once she has been carefully positioned in the ambulance. One of the crew starts up the vehicle and they're off.

"Won't put the siren on unless we have to. It tends to scare the conscious patients." The ambulance man smiles at both Philomena and Anna.

Anna moves out of the way so that the man can assess the injuries sustained by Philomena. She keeps an eye on her friend who looks at her nervously. She looks emotionally drained. The man moves away and indicates to Anna. He speaks quietly so as to be out of Philomena's hearing. "I want her to stay awake. She may have internal injuries. He stares at Anna as if trying to convey his thoughts without speaking.

Anna latches on quickly. "I'm a police officer," she whispers. "I do understand. Philomena is my flatmate and my friend. Once she's safely in the care of the hospital, I'll phone the station and let them know what's happened."

The ambulance man nods. "Keep talking to her," he tells Anna. "We don't want her falling asleep."

Luckily, it's not too far to the hospital. Anna notices that, despite the lack of a siren, other road users are very respectful of the ambulance and most pull over to let it pass.

Once at the hospital, Philomena is carefully unloaded from the ambulance and taken inside. Anna follows. Philomena is soon checked in at A&E. After a short wait, a doctor appears and gives instructions about where to take the patient. It's into a curtained off area where presumably he will examine Philomena and decide what action to take.

Meanwhile, Anna sits in the waiting area. She decides not to put in a call to the station until she knows more about Philomena's condition. Her mind is racing. Who could have done this and why ? Anna believes it must be linked to Patrick's imprisonment. Someone on the inside has got a message to someone on the outside and Philomena's attack has to be a warning when news gets back to her brother. The sooner Anna can report this to the station the better.

After a short time, the doctor emerges and two porters are called to take Philomena to a new destination. The doctor speaks to Anna who explains she is a police officer, but also a friend of the injured woman.

"She's been beaten badly. We're getting her down to x-ray to assess the damage. I've given her a dose of morphine to ease the pain in the meantime. You can stay in the visitors' room if you like and I'll keep you posted. Is there a next of kin we can contact ?"

Anna nods. "I can contact her brother". She doesn't elaborate on his whereabouts. "I also need to call the police station and get a colleague down here so that we can compose some notes about the situation. I believe the attack was linked to an ongoing case." Anna stops there.

The doctor nods and leaves, following in the direction of the trolley bearing Philomena.

In the main entrance hall of the hospital there are a number of telephone booths. Anna goes to one, dials the station number and asks the duty Sergeant if any of her team are there. It's late in the evening and she doubts it.

"No luck Anna. I can give you Frank Fernbank's home number."

Anna scrabbles in her handbag which she had grabbed at the last minute, and finds a notepad and pen.

The Sergeant reads out the number. He continues, "I'll give you Roger's number as well, in case you can't get hold of Frank."

Anna thanks him, hangs up and dials Frank's number. His wife, Mary, answers the phone. Anna apologises for phoning him at home, but Mary is obviously used to such interruptions.

Moments later, the concerned sound of Frank's voice comes on line. "What's up, Anna ?"

"Anna explains.

"Right," says her boss, "you stay put for now. Best we know the full details. If she is able to talk later, see what you can find out. OK ?"

Anna agrees.

"In the meantime, I'll alert Roger and if you get any more info, let us know asap."

"OK."

Anna returns to the visitors' room. It's empty. She picks up a magazine on a central table and opens it, but she isn't interested. She puts it back, closes her eyes and waits. She must have fallen asleep because she is awoken by a gentle nudging on her shoulder. Anna opens her eyes and looks up. She isn't sure how much time has passed.

"Your friend's out of x-ray and she's being taken to the operating theatre. Two broken ribs and some internal injuries which look as if someone, or more than one, has inflicted these injuries while she was on the ground."

The doctor pauses, giving Anna a chance to take in this awful information.

"It looks as though she was attacked and beaten and kicked." He regards Anna sympathetically. "I do hope you catch the bastards who did this."

"Don't worry. We're on it now."

"I suggest you go and get a break. Your friend will be out for the count for a while yet."

As Anna rises, he holds her arm gently. "We'll do our very best for her. Try not to worry. Good luck with your investigations."

Anna nods her thanks and moves away. She returns to the phone booths and rings the station again. She explains to the duty Sergeant that she's on her way.

"Frank and Roger are here," he tells her. "They're planning what action to take."

"Thanks Jim."

Anna goes out into the street. She feels tearful, but she knows she must be brave. Capable of investigating this crime, as she has of many others, despite her own sorrow. She remembers her dad saying, when they were speaking of the risks police officers have to take, that bravery is a skill we learn because to challenge ourselves is to grow. She has to remember this now and knows she must be strong and able to engage in seeking the villain or villains who carried out this cowardly attack on her friend.

Arriving at the station, Anna makes straight for Frank Fernbank's office.

Frank speaks first. "How is your friend ?"

Anna explains the situation and that she hasn't been able to gather any information. "I'm sure it's to do with her brother's situation. It's a warning to him not to reveal anything he knows to us and not to speak about his situation to any 'friends' who might visit."

"Do you think they might mean me ?" asks Roger. "Maybe someone got suspicious when I visited him. The trouble was he was ill at ease with me, not like he might be with a visiting friend. There were other prisoners who had visitors that day. Maybe one was a plant. If that person could read O'Farrell's body language, it probably seemed that he was nervous in my company."

"M'mm", responds Frank. He turns to Anna. "Did the doc give any indication of when Miss O'Farrell might be awake and able to speak?"

"Maybe not until morning, I should think."

"Right then. Anna, what time did your friend get home ?"

"She was due back in the early evening, but she was much later. Nearer eleven, I'd say. I phoned her friend because they went swimming after their shift at the hospital finished. That was after two this afternoon. When Philomena wasn't back by mid-evening, I rang to see if they'd been for a meal or even gone dancing. I was a bit concerned when her friend said they'd split up some hours before and as far as she knew Philomena was going to catch the train and walk back here from the station."

"I waited and then I dozed off. Around eleven she opened the front door and, well you know the rest."

"How is she ?' asks Frank.

Anna describes her injuries. Both men are horrified.

"Certainly sounds like a professional job," says Frank.

"Might even be my fault, because of the visit," says Roger, " O'Farrell was nervous with me and that might have been easy to pick up on....shit," he adds.

"Don't blame yourself," says Anna. "It could have produced results."

Roger continues to look miserable.

"Let's focus on the here and now," suggests Frank. "I want one of you to go and speak to the residents who are in the hostel. Catch them early in the morning before they leave."

"I'll do that," volunteers Anna. "Young Danny and Mick trust me and I think maybe a woman might seem less threatening to some of them. If I go early, I can also catch some of the outdoor sleepers."

"Good idea," agrees Frank. "Roger that leaves you with the shops & houses around the area of the attack. Take a couple of plods with you and speak to whoever you can. Better leave it until the morning.I think once you've got what you can from these enquiries, work together with your team. Move further afield, away from where she might have been attacked. Follow what you assume is the route back to Anna's flat. Anna, you take DC Morgan with you. Roger, use the two PCs I'll allocate. Also take DC Prentis.

Anna knows these two detectives. They are both young. DC Tim Morgan has been newly promoted to plain clothes. DC Jane Prentis has been with the team for about a year. It's now coming up to seven o'clock and the sun is rising, preparing for a long summer's day. The additional two detectives have been told to report for duty at seven. Moments later there is a knock on the door. It's DC Prentis. Close on her heels is DC Morgan.

The jobs are explained and both detectives express their sympathies to Anna. The team then split up and each pair proceeds to gather the rest of their respective team. Four early shift uniformed officers are gathered in the room used for team meetings. Their jobs are explained to them. Like their counterparts, they all tell Anna how sorry they are about what has happened to her flatmate. They all set off, determined to find the culprit or culprits responsible for this despicable attack.

---

(28) Underground & Under Cover

"I always assume a strange person that is chatting with me is an undercover police officer."

Anna had learned much about living underground and those who do so. She has learned that each underground spot in London and its outskirts offers something to the homeless and lost souls. A variety of unused stations and tunnels are used by different groups. Anna has discovered from speaking with some of the homeless residents at the hostel, who come 'up' during the day, that graffiti enthusiasts also use other abandoned parts of the Underground network. Their work is only displayed for fellow underground residents, but according to her sources is deserving of a wider audience. There are areas which offer canvases on which to create a free, yet secret, miscellany of art. Imaginative images, messages and poems adorn even the tiniest of spaces and cover the otherwise bleak walls with a new vibrancy. Anna determines to visit if and when she can. Although, chance would be a fine thing.

Anna remembers reading that during the course of the second world war, an estimated 63 million people had taken shelter in London's tube stations ! She knows that her flat-mate, Philomena has been in touch with a young homeless man called Danny. He's provided information which will be useful in the case of John Lincoln and his fraudulent commercial activities. Sadly, Philomena has explained that Danny won't meet with Anna. He will not show her where he spends his nights, as Anna is both a police officer and a woman ! All she is able to do is to ask Danny, through Philomena, to keep his eyes and ears open in case he might be able to find out something important about both the theft of the hostel's money, and the identity of anyone else involved. Although Danny appears reluctant, Anna is sure that he is, nevertheless, keen to try and help Patrick to prove his innocence. He seemed sure it wasn't a member of the homeless community who had been involved in either the theft or the attack on Philomena O'Farrell. The latter had been printed on the front pages of most of the morning's newspapers. Anna determines to speak to the officer who is about to go undercover. He's young and he might be able to befriend Danny. It would be a foot in the door for entry into this whole 'otherworld'.

At the station on this bright summer's morning, the teams leading the investigation into the theft of the homeless charity's funds and the subsequent imprisonment of Patrick O'Farrell and now the attack on his sister are busy at work.

Frank Fernbank has news for them. He reminds them that the Criminal Intelligence Branch covering 'Covert Policing' is a branch of the police force. It was formed in March 1960 and provides advice and rules about surveillance on known criminals. 'God' (Superintendent Victor Jenkins) upstairs has emphasised to Frank and his teams this approach is designed to keep pace with modern criminal methodology and technology. Frank has been advised that many, even most, of his officers at Woodstone nick were known to both customers and staff of the hostel.

"As a result of this, you may both be disappointed to know that God and the Powers that be, have decided that the undercover officer suggested is to be provided by the Met. His name is Ben Miller. A PC. He's only 20 years old, a bright lad who has been chosen because of his age and, all being well, his ability to mix with the residents of the hostel, especially younger lads like Danny." Fernbank looks at Anna & winks. "He's a keen lad but it's a risky job. In light of that we are going to give him every support, all the back-up, we can. Under no circumstances will PC Miller come to this station. He's keeping his surname, Miller, with a first name of Paul. If you happen to come across him, you DO NOT approach him. Just report it to me. Ben will report to his station when he can. He'll use a public phone box for any emergencies. There might be a few grumbles about the choice of an officer from another area, but in general everyone will know it makes sense. Most street and underground dwellers know members of the local nick here."

Anna has been reading up on police documents which discuss fraud and how it can be detected. She discovers it's a growing problem and overall she guesses that the fraud she and her workmates are investigating is small in comparison to other examples. Nevertheless, it's the situation with Patrick which needs sorting out and Anna wants to approach the situation from both a professional and a personal perspective.

She is shocked to discover that tampering schemes, expense reimbursement schemes and payroll schemes are all common in the modern workplace. More than half of dishonest employees create fraudulent documents to cover their tracks, apparently. Others alter documents, create fraudulent journal entries, or simply 'cook the books'.

Those who are in debt or living beyond their means are more likely to commit fraud. Small-business owners and charities are more vulnerable to internal theft than big companies and may not be able to cover the losses.

As in this charity case, internal theft can be difficult to detect. Warning signs should be watched out for. Payroll discrepancies, missing inventories or a sudden drop in available funds should raise a red flag. Anna realises that in the case of the hostel, although the Manager is the most likely suspect. Possibly, with the help of others, but that's more difficult to prove, unless the boss spills the beans. For Anna, this example of theft is more despicable because the hostel is run as a charity. Donors and volunteers are being cheated, not to mention the homeless ones themselves.

This example of internal theft involves stealing money that has already been recorded in a company's books. Like other fraud schemes, it can take many forms, such as altering cash accounts and stealing cash. In the hostel's case, theft was made easier because it was mainly the Manager who handled the money. Anna guessed volunteers might be bribed, but that seemed unlikely as these people wanted to help the homeless community and were unlikely to be thieves, unless they had been planted there by the Manager.

Anna goes on to learn that cash skimming frauds are another form of theft and could go undetected for quite a time when the person in charge was the thief ! This type of fraud involves stealing cash before it's recorded in the company's books. Sometimes, it involves the theft of cheques. In the hostel's case, cash from collection boxes would be an easy target.

One investigation area that Frank Fernbank has allocated to Anna and Roger is checking when any losses had been noticed or reported. If revenues suddenly dropped by an unusual amount, perhaps this could be pointed out by another member of staff, especially a regular volunteer. For instance, not giving receipts to customers who pay in cash. The money goes into the pocket, or pockets, of the culprit/s. instead of into the cash register. Since these donations are not recorded, the fraud is hard to detect.

Once the investigators are able to identify potential suspects, they must find someone on the inside to take proactive action and double-check the records for anything suspicious. That way, the suspect has less opportunity to suss out they have been under surveillance.

The next morning Roger, Anna and their two colleagues have a team meeting. Both Anna and Roger discuss their own ideas about how to go about the investigation.

Anna outlines her thoughts and shares the research she has done.

Roger comes up with an interesting way forward. "I've discovered that much of the initial money for founding the hostel and finding suitable premises was provided by a businessman called Raymond Merryweather. Apparently, he came from a poor background himself and determined once he had made much money in the investment banking sector, that he would find a way of helping those who had fallen on hard times. Helping the homeless seemed a good way forward. Unfortunately for them, Raymond Merryweather died some years before.

Anna and Roger have been instructed to look at the issue of the suspect using friends or relatives to work at the hostel. This could raise the alarm .

"Let's see if there are regular cash counts and that the company's bank accounts have been checked every month. " suggests Roger.

"Good idea," agrees Anna. "Does another outside party review their financial statements on a monthly basis? Do they use an accountant and if they do we can ask him to assess the likelihood of fraud ? From what I've been reading, investigation of all discrepancies, no matter how small or insignificant they may seem, is a way forward. Maybe opening the door to other wrongdoing."

"You're right," agrees Roger.

(29) Onward & Downward

"Once well underground, you know exactly where you are. Nothing can happen to you, and nothing can get at you. You're entirely your own

master and you don't have to consult anybody or mind what they say. Things go on all the same overhead, and you let 'em, and don't bother about 'em. When you want to, up you go, and there the things are, waiting for you."

(Kenneth Grahame, The Wind in the Willows)

It's PC Ben (alias Paul) Miller's first foray into the homeless and underground community. It's also his first time undercover and he's scared and excited in equal measure. As a keen biker, excitement comes through starting his mental engine and hearing and feeling the purr of anticipation.

Ben (Paul) enters the hostel at the end of the afternoon where he discovers it's meal time. As he enters the building the smell of cooking meets his nose. Things look busy. It's a hive of activity with men of all ages queuing for their supper. As the queue moves forward and men take a seat, Tom joins the end of the line. He notices several puzzled glances. He's hoping to meet the older man who had been robbed and, all being well, Danny. Anna had provided a description of Danny. He was aged about 18 and was tall and thin. He had very blonde hair, pale skin and blue eyes. Paul's eye examines the people queuing. He looks, but tries not to stare. There is a young man matching the description of Danny that he's been given at the front of the queue. Paul watches carefully to suss out where this man sits. Danny moves to the far corner of the room, as if trying to not make himself look noticeable.

Paul collects his food and wanders casually over to the table where Danny has begun eating.

"Mind if I sit here ?" he asks, standing by a chair opposite Danny.

Danny looks up and shrugs his shoulders. Paul sits down.

"Not bad nosh," observes Paul, taking a mouthful.

Danny remains silent.

Paul continues eating in silence for a while.

D'you come here a lot ?" Paul asks Danny.

Danny doesn't look up but continues his meal. He stays quiet.

Paul perseveres. "It's my first time here. Someone told me about it. I was pretty hungry, so this is great."

Danny looks up briefly, but doesn't speak. It's as if Paul had been speaking a language he couldn't understand. Danny finishes his meal, and leaves the table without looking back. Paul is frustrated, but he knows he has to be patient. Danny and others like him may have had bad experiences with other people, especially those they didn't know.

Danny has taken his crockery and cutlery to a trolley where used dishes are being collected. He leaves the room. Paul has an urge to follow him, but he knows that would be the wrong move. Normally he likes to jump in at the deep end, but he knows in this instance, he has to be patient and take it slowly.

Paul gets up and heads to the trolley with his dirty dishes.

As he does so an older man approaches him. "No good trying to make friends with that little bastard, he's a miserable sod !"

Paul nods his understanding.

The man continues chatting. "Not seen you here before ?"

"No….I had a bit of trouble somewhere else, so I decided to move on."

"Well, you've landed on your feet here my lad. They look after you…." He pauses and looks round. No-one else is nearby. In a whisper, he tells Paul, "Just watch out for thieves. There's some here you can't trust and…." He looks around to check no-one is earwigging. "…it's not us lot, it's them as is in charge." He gestures in the direction of the office…."You've been warned lad."

"Thanks," responds Paul. This is music to his ears. He's not going to push it today by asking too many questions, but he's beginning to feel he's got a foot in the door.

The next thing he needs to focus on is finding his way into an underground shelter.

---

(30) Where are They ?

"What I have always found is, anything one keeps hidden should now and then be hidden somewhere else."

(Elizabeth Bowen, The Death of the Heart)

In an abandoned space, under part of the Victorian railway line in East London there are archways leading to open spaces. Some are used for storage, often of items that had fallen off the back of lorries. Two men approach one of the archways which has a solid wooden door closed by a huge padlock. The first man produces an equally large key and opens the door. Inside is dirty. The filth of decades hangs from the walls. Cobwebs are rampant. Each day, the building is treated to a fresh layer of grime from the passing steam trains.

One man lights a large torch and amongst the shadows, several wooden crates can be seen lining the back wall of the building. Inside are packets of drugs. For the addicts who acquire them, an easy road to hell. For the dealers a massive profit. Drug dealing has become much more prevalent in the last few years. The two men standing in this cave, have one aim, that is to make money from selling drugs. They are competing in a ruthless market where drug buying and taking is normalised. For these two, what began as a way of making an additional income has become a major undertaking. More risky, as more users become hooked and the use of drugs quickly becomes widepread.

As the problem grows, it has become clear that old legislation relating to drug use had to be updated. A few years earlier, the Conservative MP Sir Hugh Linstead had tabled a Private Members Bill that was passed as the Dangerous Drugs Act 1964. It sought to quell growing concerns of the societal effects of the cultivation and usage of cannabis. In Britain, since the war, there had been a huge increase in criminal offences for possession of the drug with surveys suggesting that a great number of undergraduate students were users. As the problem grew, in the same year Parliament also passed the Drugs (Prevention of Misuse) Act, outlawing the sale of amphetamines which had been linked to a rise in juvenile delinquency. Only the previous year, the Dangerous Drugs Act 1965 had been drafted in accordance with the 1961 United Nations Convention on Narcotic Drugs, consolidating previous drugs legislation. This meant that drug dealing was dodgier, but also more lucrative for the likes of the two men in the space which had become their drug store.

John Lincoln, an ex-public schoolboy, had been training as an accountant before the war broke out. The City bank he worked for had taught him well. After the war, returning to a job as an accountant seemed totally uninviting. He had been 30 years old and didn't plan to stay in such a mundane role for over thirty years until he retired to Brighton !

Then drugs came on the scene. Lincoln read about drug dealers making a fortune. He had to find a job where he could be in charge of money which could then be rerouted. He saw an advertisement in the local paper. Maybe drug addicts might be among the homeless customers who used the facilities at the 'Help the Homeless' charity. Maybe the trustees of such a charity would leave the day to day management of monies to the Manager. He went for an interview. His public school education, combined with his military service, impressed the trustees of the charity and he was offered the post on the spot.

John Lincoln hadn't rushed. 'Everything comes to he who waits, he told himself. After only a month, he had settled into the job and in addition to his attempts to find customers for drugs, he also found that the trustees had put their total trust in his ability to organise and manage the donations that the charity received.

Lincoln soon found ways of 'cooking the books' so that money destined for the charity could be transferred into a special bank account he had set up. From this account he was able to transfer funds into an overseas bank account. In turn, this money could be transferred into another bank account that he had set up in Spain.

Over a period of time, he discussed ideas with Reg Houghton. They discovered that drug trafficking is now a major source of revenue for organised crime groups. Many of these gangs are already involved in other forms of serious crime. Because neither Lincoln nor Houghton had criminal records, it was unlikely, provided they were cautious, that they would be found out. Reg Houghton, it turned out, had some friends involved in crime. One of these in particular, was a bloke known as Jack Jones, who he knew had begun to dabble in drug dealing. For Jones, it was merely a sideline and it seemed he hadn't done much research. A mate had approached him about selling cannabis. Amongst other activities, Jack Jones ran a market stall on Petticoat Lane. Most of his stock had been obtained through suspect sources. 'Ladies and gentlemen's clothing straight from the Paris catwalk.' he would claim aloud. All Jack Jones had to do was wait until a customer asked about the pockets on garments. Jack would reach out for a jacket he had kept 'behind the counter' He would then offer up the garment for the customer to try on. The customer would admire himself in the mirror provided, whilst surreptitiously removing a small package from the pocket of the jacket. He would then return the jacket saying he didn't think it suited him. In the other pocket of the jacket was payment for the drugs. The deal was done.

When Reg Houghton had related this arrangement to John Lincoln, the latter had an idea. "Why pay for the drugs and then act as middlemen ? Why don't we investigate the source of the 'goods' and buy direct ? More money in our pockets and less chance of being caught. Plus, we can buy larger quantities once we establish a wider range of customers."

Reg Houghton had agreed and then revealed his ownership of the perfect hiding place under the railway arches.

---

(31) Exploring the Depths

"A place not of moments, but moment. A waiting place."

(Nicole T. Smith, We Have Shadows Too)

In the two weeks he has been frequenting the hostel, any budding relationship with Danny had proved elusive. However, Ben (Paul) has managed to speak to Arthur, the older man who was sure some of his money was being stolen from his bag. Not stolen every night, but on several occasions over a period of time. Arthur was a bit vague about how long this period was.

"One day's much the same as another," he admits. "Mind you, I'm coming here for meals now, but I spend most of my nights underground."

Paul's ears prick up at this revelation. Could this be his opportunity to find an opening into the underground community ?

" Arthur looks pensive. "Trouble is kid, when I'm pissed, I can't remember anything. It's only later that I find out my money has been nicked. Never all of it. They know I'd kick up more of a fuss. As far as most people are concerned I'm just an old wino talking bollocks."

"Yeah, but that's not right," sympathises Paul.

"Life ain't right," says Arthur wistfully. "He studies Paul's face. "Anyhow, what's a youngster like you doing on the streets ?"

Paul's ready with an answer. "Mum and dad chucked me out. I was 15 and got caught doing a bit of pilfering at our local corner shop. The owner called the cops. After a discussion they let me off with a warning. Mum and dad were so ashamed. Then I was out on my ear."

"Couldn't they have helped ?" asks Arthur.

"Dad sees himself as a 'pillar of the community'. They're both religious too. Devout Catholics. No second chances……although I think the decision was mainly dad's, but mum goes along with anything he says."

"Pity," sympathises Arthur.

"I'm not a criminal. I'm trying to get a job. You know, bank messenger or something like that. Got to make a bit of money though. I can't even afford any decent clothes to go for an interview. "

Arthur is thoughtful. "I know a bloke who deals in secondhand clothes. I'm sure he could rustle up something for you."

"How can I contact him ?" asks Paul. Could this be his chance to meet someone from Underground ?

"I'd have to speak to him first. Vouch for you as it were before he'll deal with a stranger."

Paul immediately feels guilty. He's not who Arthur thinks he is. But hey, that's part of the job, he tells himself.

Arthur adds, "I'll see if he's coming here for a meal soon. Then, I can introduce you."

"Thanks."

Paul leaves the hostel and wanders through the streets. As Ben, he knows the goal he's set himself is good for him and good for solving the case as well. It feels as if a fire has been lit inside. It's a fire that feels like pleasure. It makes his undercover task feel exciting. Here, out of uniform, he is free to develop his persona as Paul. He's on a path and it's the right path. Goal setting from within is like a fuel of freedom, a need that fulfils his objectives. This is real police work ! Ben's police instinct, though, tells him not to push things at this stage. He needs to get in touch with Danny, but also ensure that he himself is recognised and accepted as part of the community before taking any action. Danny might begin to trust 'Paul' if he becomes accepted as a regular at the hostel. Time to report back to HQ with an update on his progress. 'Slowly, slowly catchee monkey', he tells himself.

---

(32) Lincoln On the Move

"You must actively manage your career because otherwise things won't just happen. Hope is not a strategy."

(Binod Shankar, Let's Get Real: 42 Tips for the Stuck Manager)

It's Friday afternoon and Anna has received a phone call from a frantic Janet. She arranges to call at the Hostel for the Homeless immediately.

Upon entering, it's clear Janet is very anxious. Anna suggests she sits down and takes a deep breath before she explains the reason for her call.

Janet nervously takes a deep breath and begins. "John Lincoln, as you know he's the Manager of the hostel, has told us, just us at the end of the lunch hour, that he's off on two weeks' holiday. He's leaving Maureen, who's worked there for ages, in charge. I don't think she's involved in any theft of money. She's not the brightest spark, bless her, so it would have been easy for Mr Lincoln to pull the wool over her eyes."

Anna is shocked by this revelation. "When's he leaving ?"

"Tonight, I think. he's flying to Spain."

Anna's mind goes into overdrive. If Lincoln is the thief, then he could disappear and never return. "Can I use your phone ?" she asks Janet.

Janet nods agreement.

Anna phones the station. Luckily, Frank is still there. As soon as she gets through to him, the words tumble from her mouth like a waterfall.

"Bloody hell," exclaims Frank. "I'll get onto London Airport police and get him stopped." He looks at his watch. 5.30pm. He speaks to Anna again. "What time did he leave the hostel ?"

Anna consults Janet. "He left early. After lunch. 2 ish.

"Leave it with me and get back here pronto," instructs Frank.

---

(33) Report From Below

"Great things are done by a series of small things brought together."

(Vincent Van Gogh)

Ben (Paul) has reported back with his progress. He's been praised for his efforts and encouraged to take the next step and meet with the man who lives underground. He's named Harry. Rumour has it that he was once an academic, a historian, who became a drinker and was eventually given the sack on the QT from his university. They clearly wanted to avoid adverse publicity. It's said that he is very clever, has recovered more or less from his alcoholism and now acts as a father figure to some of the younger homeless. Like Arthur, he is respected throughout the homeless community and has become known as The Invisible Man as he manages to move from place to place above ground, never staying on the same pitch, but still remaining in the locality around his home. Apparently, Harry tells tales of how the sociopolitical rulers of the country now reject his academic contributions to the history of the country. As a result, he is obliged to 'hibernate' as he calls it.

Arthur proves to be as good as his word. Ben (Paul) is told he can visit the underground hideout, but he has to keep the location and the name of the person he will be dealing with highly secret.

They meet one evening at the hostel. After a meal, Arthur tells Paul that he is leaving. Paul must stay put for five minutes or so and then follow. They would meet up on The Flats, opposite the Robin Hood pub. "There's a little copse of trees there, explains Arthur.. I'll meet you round the back of it, under the trees. That way we shouldn't be seen."

Paul nods. He waits. Once Arthur has left, Paul finishes his cup of tea and then takes his plate and mug to the trolley on his way out. Once outside, he begins walking. He stops a couple of times to look in a shop window. That gives him time to check he isn't being followed. It takes him about ten minutes to reach The Flats. Sure enough, hiding behind a tree, he spots Arthur.

Arthur directs him to follow. They cross The Flats, walking away from the town centre. They emerge on a suburban street and follow it to a roundabout. Arthur turns left. As he does so, Paul notices, on the same side of the road, what was once a London Underground station. The words 'Wood Lane' can still be read on a long since rusted sign, attached to the front of the building. There are barred gates making access unlikely, if not impossible. Arthur leads Paul along a narrow passageway. Emerging, they turn right. The back of the station greets them. The walls are still firm. The roof has holes where the tiles have fallen or broken. A battered door with peeling paint is locked and partially covered by weeds. Arthur produces a key and places it in a semi-hidden padlock. Arthur is known to Harry, the 'father-figure' of the underground community. Arthur produces a key from his pocket and opens the padlock on the door. Moments later, a voice can be heard on the other side of the door.

"Password ?"

"Helter-skelter," says Arthur, clearly and confidentlly.

"You may enter," says the voice.

The sound of bolts being drawn back can be heard. They step inside.

The voice materialises into a man of about Arthur's age. Paul realises this must be Harry. The map of wrinkles on his face tells of the longest and troubled journey through life. Yet, the lines around his eyes also tell of laughter, of warm smiles and affection. His forehead speaks of worries past and present. The lines are deeply ingrained. They tell of a man who has travelled through maybe six or more decades up until this moment. He stands here as an old man, seemingly beaten and forlorn. Paul has the feeling that in society he is dismissed as "old", yet he is likely much more than the sum of his physical parts. Paul is beginning to realise that he could say the same of Arthur, albeit that he is most likely younger. Life on the streets is hard.

The man greets Arthur and then looks at Paul suspiciously. "Who's this ?" he asks roughly.

Arthur puts his hand on Tom's shoulder. "This is Paul, Harry."

Harry regards Paul without speaking for a moment. Then Arthur speaks. "Paul's been using the 'Help the Homeless' hostel. Was a runaway once, now living on the streets."

The man looks him up and down. "You're lucky to have found Arthur and I hope his faith in you is not misplaced."

Paul smiles what he hopes is seen as a polite gesture.

Harry continues. "This place has become a home for those who need a place to thrive and live better lives. We, I mean the homeless, have made new communities in places such as this. We rebuild them. Rescued buildings rescue people. What might have been thought of as a derelict society, here has become something beautiful, sustainable and good in the truest sense. You, young Paul, are privileged and, to begin with, on probation. I hope Arthur's trust is warranted."

Ben, as Paul, feels his cheeks turning scarlet. He doesn't like to think what might become of him if they find he has deceived them. Still, he has to put that to one side for the time being. Concentrate on the job in hand.

---

(34) A Falling Out Amongst Thieves

"When thieves fall out, the thefts come to light."

Spanish proverb

John Lincoln had, some weeks before trying to escape the country, read about the murder of a young man in the newspaper. He hadn't thought much about it. However, one morning he was on his way to see Reg Houghton at his garage. As he arrived, he was in time to see Reg emerging from the garage with another man. The second man is shouting at Reg and there's clearly an argument going on. The man returns to his car, slams the door and drives away, tyres screeching as he does so. Lincoln waits until the man has driven away, then goes into the garage to find Reg Houghton. He finds his partner in crime, red-faced and furious.

"What's up ?" enquiries Lincoln.

"Dissatisfied customer," replies Reg Houghton.

John Lincoln is concerned. The response doesn't ring true. "Come on Reg. What have you been up to ? Remember, we have been working together. I don't want you buggering up our 'arrangement'.

Reg is red-faced. He looks angry. "Who the hell do you think you are ? Interfering in my affairs."

"As long as it's not OUR affairs, Reg !" John Lincoln is getting angry and suspicious.

"Piss off !" exclaims Houghton.

"You'd better cool down. Meet me at the 'warehouse' later. We need to discuss this further."

Reg Houghton doesn't reply. He is losing self control. "Maybe" he mutters to the departing figure. He stomps back to his office. He can't help thinking about the fate of young Tom Preston. He reckoned Tom had become suspicious about what was going on. He had a good eye and a sharp intellect. Reg had wanted him given a warning through a beating. Trust that idiot, Dave, to go over the top. He'd read the newspaper accounts about the body found in Epping forest. Dave had obviously taken that bloody dog with him. Hence the ludicrous wolf attack stories in the newspapers. What had he done ? He is feeling panicked.

John Lincoln is worried. He has a perfect arrangement going on. Drugs and fiscal fraud are making him a very rich man. Reg Houghton is a moron. Why the hell did he get mixed up with him ? He's a loser. He could do for them both……Maybe if he turns up at the 'warehouse' tonight he might just get more than he bargained for ! Better if his partnership with Houghton was ended. He remembers the revolver he had taken from a German soldier captured during the war now lying in a drawer at home, unused for many years. What if ?...........

Lincoln decides to take time out to think things through. He needs to be surrounded by others in a place where he belongs. For him, that is The Regency Club. There, he can be peaceful and have time to think and plan. He prides himself on being a member of the club. It's his church, the place where he senses the energy of belonging in every atom. This is the reality of his world. Other chaps don't interfere. They understand. Getting what you want allows for some unorthodox measures. He should never have trusted a yob like Reg Houghton. It was a mistake. 'Well Reg,' he whispers to the ether, 'you're going to get your comeuppance.'

John Lincoln sits in his private room and orders a brandy to be delivered to him. Once that has happened, he phones Reg. "Look Reg, we need to talk things over. Sort out any problems !" He gives a haughty laugh. Silence at the other end of the phone. "How about meeting me at the warehouse. We'll sort things out there and then. Then we'll both know where we are, eh ?"

Reg hesitates. He consults his watch and replies sulkily, "I can be there around seven."

"Perfect," replies John. He replaces the receiver and smirks like the cat who got the cream.

Shortly before 7 that evening, John Lincoln arrives at the 'warehouse'. For him, morality has become nothing more than a sophistry to deliver the most basic, selfish wants of the human psyche. He has the patter. He's a silver-tongued devil who reigns over his kingdom. Reg is now obsolete, in his way, so he must be removed. It's as simple as that. He has loaded his revolver. He's ready. He's nervous. His hand shakes a little as he handles the weapon. He tells himself that it's natural to be nervous. In fact, he says to himself, he'd be more concerned if he wasn't anxious or nervous. After all, there's all the difference in the world between brave and being foolish. 'I'm brave', he told himself. 'It's good. It makes me feel more reliable and solid.' It was as if greed had manifested itself into his hands as a pistol. It was that genocidal impulse that once brought to life is always ready and waiting. Greed being magnified and satisfied by violence.

He hears the sound of a car pulling up and then the door being slammed shut. Reg is here. He's walking towards the door. Lincoln primes the gun. He stands back from the door, ready to fire. Reg Houghton sees John Lincoln's car and notices the padlock on the warehouse door is open. He walks towards the entrance. He doesn't feel any unease. As he pushes the door open, he just has time to take in the scene before him. John Lincoln holding a revolver. Reg is frozen to the spot. He should move but he can't. There's a fatal attraction to the scene before him.

The gun fires. It flies like a guided missile. As it reaches its target, Reg Houghton crumples like a straw-filled scarecrow. The final expression on his face is a mix of puzzlement and surprise.

(35) The Great Escape

We feel free when we escape - even if it be but from the frying pan to the fire.

(Eric Hoffer)

John Lincoln decides to leave Reg's body where it lies. The warehouse is well-hidden from view from the road. Anyway, most users of the spaces there are up to no good ! He moves the body to the back of the building and pushed a couple of empty wooden chests in front of it.

Now, he is on the road. He knows now he should have followed his instincts. Not only has he had to dispose of that bastard, Reg Houghton, but to add fuel to the fire, he has discovered that the bloody woman, Janet, at the Help the Homeless' charity has been mouthing off to the police. Looking back, he realises that she'd been behaving strangely for a while. He realises now that it was his own arrogance that had dismissed the idea of her sussing out what he was up to. Panic switches off your higher brain function, he tells himself. Think straight and start thinking about solutions. He curses himself for being careless. He'd deluded himself into imagining he is invincible. What a careless idiot he'd been. Too clever for his own good ! Anyway, now, he is doing the right thing. As soon as he heard her on the phone to God knows who, maybe the police, he knew it was time to get out.

Before meeting Reg, he'd gathered his belongings from the office. He'd thought about going via home. No, he'd phone the airport from his desk right there and then. He taps his foot impatiently as the girl who answers the phone goes to check the next flight to Marbella. When she returns to the phone, he is relieved to hear there is a flight at 6.30pm that evening and there is space for him.

"Would you like to book that now, sir ?" the girl had asked.

He had sighed with relief as he'd said yes. He looked at his watch. He wondered again if it was worth chancing a trip to his home ? No, if Maggie, his wife, was there, it would be too complicated. She isn't part of his plans. Luckily, he had already transferred the bulk of his money into a Spanish bank account. A healthy fortune awaits him in Spain.

He is so hyped up he suddenly realises he's driving like a mad man. He doesn't care about the other traffic that screeches, swerves and honks around him. He is like a speeding arrow heading straight for its target.

In the meantime, Frank Fernbank has alerted the airport police. A description of John Lincoln and his car has been circulated to all available police cars.

Lincoln continues his mad dash. He crosses junctions at red lights and screeches round bends so fast it seems as though his car might turn over and career off the road. Although it's summer time, the daylight is hiding. He is aware of his surroundings only as dark silhouettes hidden by a thick mist as he races by. The road is the only light, directing him and stretching into the gloom. He scans for cars following. There are none. Now, he's leaving the city. The traffic thins a little.

He relaxes into the drive, a smirk forming on his face. The rumble of traffic quietens. As he continues, he sees a sign directing him to London Airport. He turns the wheel. It's in that moment that a smirk develops on his face. Nearly there. No need to panic. Fate has tipped the balance in his favour.

---

(36) Philomena Returns

"To move forward, you have to return home."

(Rita Marley)

Philomena is being released from hospital today. Anna has arranged some time off work to collect her flatmate from the hospital and return her home. When Anna arrives, she is directed to a small, empty waiting room where Philomena is seated. She has a bag at her side which contains toiletries and other essentials which Anna had brought her from home. As soon as the door opens, Philomena looks up, catches Anna's eye and stands up. Anna senses that she looks relieved. In her mind, Philomena is thinking that returning home is more a sensation of the heart than of physical location. Although the thought of her own room and her own bed is alive and kicking. She hugs Anna.

"Thanks for coming. I can't tell you how glad I am to be coming home. The staff here have been great. I can't complain, but there's nothing like home."

Anna smiles. She is pleased that Philomena feels that her flatshare is really like 'home', even though she's only been there for a matter of months. Anna picks up the bag and steers Philomena towards the door. Philomena asks to leave via the nurses' station so that she can offer thanks for their care.

They're driving home. Anna feels that although it would be tempting to question Philomena to try and elicit more information about her attackers, she decides to wait until her friend is settled in and relaxed. Once she has settled in there will be time for questioning.

Once back at the flat, Anna carries the bag and opens the door. She has put up some 'welcome home' balloons which make Philomena smile. Anna proceeds to make a cup of tea.

"Do you want anything to eat ? Maybe a light lunch ? I bought some salad and nice fresh bread from the baker's."

Philomena smiles as she flops onto the sofa. She looks around as if familiarising herself with the flat all over again. "No, just tea would be great."

They drink their tea. Then Anna announces, "I have to go back to work, but I'll be back around teatime. Are you going to be OK ? My mum volunteered to come and keep you company if you like."

"That's kind, but I'll just rest. Just before you go, could you get a book from my bag ? Don't laugh, it's a detective novel !"

Anna reaches into the bag and discovers the book entitled "The Forest Murders' by J.P. Digby. "Cheerful stuff !" She grins and hands the book over. "See you later. You can ring mum or me if there's any problem. Lock the door when I'm gone…..just to be on the safe side," she adds.

Philomena follows Anna to the door and, as requested, locks it behind her. She feels uncomfortable doing it, but she knows it's sensible. She doesn't want to focus on her attack, so she sits with her feet up on the sofa to discover more about the fictional 'Forest Murders'. The phone is on a side table where she can reach it.

Anna is wary of leaving Philomena alone, but she'll be back in a few hours.

---

(37) The Chase is On

"We must learn to sail in high winds."

Aristotle Onassis

Anna and Roger are in a police car driven by PC Sam Grant, a trained police driver, used to chases, or getting urgently to a crime scene. In this case it's en route to London Airport's departures building to catch John Lincoln before his flight leaves. Anna finds the journey exhilarating. PC Sam Grant knows that the driving involves keeping his wits about him.

He has acquired a sense of tunnel vision which keeps him firmly on track. He is very conscious of the hazard of the pursuit itself, especially through the congested streets of the capital. He has to constantly avoid a collision between the racing vehicle of the patrol car and the danger of becoming involved in an accident with an innocent driver or pedestrian. It's his duty to constantly weigh the risk of the chase against the gravity of the reason for it.

At the moment, he knows that John Lincoln has put some distance between him and his pursuers. He is far enough ahead not to need to respond to the police car's lights and siren. If Sam Grant allows himself to be sucked in by the excitement of the pursuit, he could make mistakes. He has to avoid an overreaction. He knows that another police car is following and the airport police will be ready and waiting. In fact, they may have nabbed Lincoln before he can escape.

Some distance ahead, Lincoln has abandoned his car in the car park and is heading for the Departures area. As PC Grant pulls into the Airport car park, there is no sign of the car, which he had earlier discovered over the radio is a Pale blue Ford Zodiac.

"Shall I drive round the car park and have a look ?" asks Sam.

"No, stop at the entrance doors and leave the car there," instructs Roger. "Anna and I will go inside and you stay with the car and keep your eyes peeled."

When Anna and Roger enter the Departures area it is quite busy. Flight desks are open and people are queuing to check in and place their luggage ready to be taken onto the waiting plane, a Vickers Viscount, soon to be heading for Marbella in Spain.

Roger pushes his way towards a departures desk, holding up his police ID and saying loudly, "Police". Surprised passengers step back to let him through. The woman behind the counter looks at him nervously.

"Have you seen this man," asks Roger, holding up a photograph of John Lincoln.

"The woman shakes her head nervously.

Both Anna and Roger turn sharply as a door on the other side of the departure area is pushed open and three airport police officers appear, firmly holding the arms of a man who has been handcuffed.

"He's been cautioned," explains one of the officers as they head towards Anna and Roger who are holding up their ID cards.

John Lincoln doesn't make eye contact with either of them. He looks past them with angry eyes. He has switched gear from the fake empathy he had shown as Manager of the Help the Homeless hostel. His face now portrays cold, emotional indifference. He directs this expression to where Anna and Roger are waiting. He senses they are a threat. He goes into full self protective mode. He wants to be in control, but he knows deep down that the game is up.

---

(38) Exposing the Fraud

"Rather fail with honour than succeed by fraud. "

(Sophocles)

Anna had been sent on a course on the subject of drug abuse. She has also been reading up on the subject of the drugs' trade. It's one terrible price to pay for its victims, she concludes. She thinks angrily about John Lincoln and others like him who contribute to wrecking people's lives by feeding their addiction. Money was the god to these traffickers. She has learned that as well as drug trafficking, the whole dreadful business could involve child trafficking, prostitution and drug factory slave labour. Many questions run through her head. Who is really paying the consequences for this trade system? Thinking about young people and the homeless, she wonders what they are paying with ? What does it cost them ? She strongly feels that police officers need the new training which is coming on board. We must be willing to shine lights in the darkest of places, she believes. Increasing the real action required to stop it is indeed the responsibility of the police, in conjunction with those working in the social services. It breaks her heart to think that it's always the most vulnerable who are most likely to be the victims.

As soon as Lincoln had been detained, everything began to unravel. One of the trustees, a Brian Carter, has arrived at Woodstone police station, together with Janet Gardner.

They are invited into an interview room. Brian Carter explains to Anna and Frank that on a visit to the hostel that he had recently asked John Lincoln whether he had managed to recoup monies paid on an invoice that they noticed he had already paid twice two years ago.

"Knowing that I worked in accounts," says Brian Carter, "the trustees asked me to try and unravel the mystery. I searched the documentation. To my amazement, I found that in the situation I was investigating, Mr Lincoln had paid the second amount to himself by cheque. Each cheque has to be countersigned by a trustee , but in this case, Mr Lincoln had forged the signature of the senior trustee, Mr Wilson. The evidence was there in black and white."

"So what happened next ?" asks Anna.

" I reported it to the other trustees and an emergency meeting was called. At that meeting, the senior trustee, Mr Williams, and I recommended an immediate investigation on suspicion of gross misconduct. on Mr Lincoln's part."

Frank asks, "so, you think Lincoln cottoned on to the fact he was going to be found out ?"

"In retrospect, yes. I don't mind saying it's become even more of a shattering experience. The trustees have since held the urgent meeting to look for more proof. They've looked at every single transaction going back over the five years that Mr Lincoln has been in his job. It transpires that he has repeatedly stolen thousands of pounds by writing cheques to himself. He has fabricated expenses and pocketed the petty cash. I mentioned to the trustee that there had even been suspicions mentioned by some of the homeless men who use the hostel. One in particular who was sure Mr Lincoln had stolen money from his bag when he stayed at the hostel overnight."

Janet looks increasingly miserable. Anna can see she's close to tears. She looks at Anna for reassurance and Anna smiles. " I've been speaking to the regulars at the hostel," explains Janet. "They have also long suspected that Mr Lincoln had even pilfered takings from the residents, but none of them were sure. there was no proof."

Anna senses Janet is getting more upset. "No-one is blaming you Janet."

Brian Carter adds, "we need to contact the Charity Commission to alert them to these goings-on".

Anna is sorry for Janet and feels anger for all the homeless people who have been deprived of funds that would have benefitted them.

Shortly afterwards, PC Lily Saunders enters with three cups of tea.

Anna begins, thanking Janet for her help so far. "I've put Detective Chief Inspector Fernbank in the picture," explains Anna, "so you can start from where we left off before."

Janet smiles nervously and takes a sip of her tea. " I have been assisting the trustees with collecting proof of Mr Lincoln's guilt. Maureen, my co-worker, and I carried on digging. We got increasingly worried when we found a history of cover-ups and mismanagement. We reported straight to the trustees. It was discovered that the fraudulent transactions coincided with the appointment of Mr Lincoln."

Brian Carter nodded. "The cash flow and the profit and loss figures he has been producing are, for want of a better word, rubbish. Cheques he claimed to have issued had in fact never been sent. It's basically a huge and complicated mess that will take our entire attention for months,.... to the detriment of other tasks I'm afraid."

Janet is looking tearful. Her face is red with emotion. "I feel sad and angry at the same time. As if those homeless people hadn't suffered enough. I still find it hard to believe that he could have got away with it for so long. As Maureen said, we tend to trust people working for charities……maybe I'm just naive….." A tear ran down her cheek and she hung her head, as if she was to blame.

Anna reassures her that it wasn't her fault.

Brian Carter chips in, "after all, Janet, even the trustees have been fooled. "

Frank adds, "If he can be found guilty and it seems plenty of evidence has been revealed, the case will eventually come to court. That will take time though. In the meantime, we need to continue to gather as much proof as possible. The more proof we have, the better the chance of a conviction for fraud."

Anna makes eye contact with Janet and smiles at her. "You're doing a good thing, believe me."

Janet nods cautiously.

Brian Carter says, "we've taken a deep breath and written a formal letter to our key business donors. The press are banging at our door and large donors had to be warned in advance of the press coverage. Otherwise, I fear they will abandon us."

"Frank speaks. "I think that's a wise move. We appreciate you can't leave things in limbo."

Janet smiles and seems relieved. "To my relief, I'm pleased to say that those donors who have so far replied have done so with sympathy. Some even shared similar experiences in other charities, or heard of similar cases. I suppose that was meant to make me feel better. Trouble is it's making me cynical. Who can you trust ?" Janet retrieves a handkerchief from her handbag and dabs her eyes.

Neither Anna nor Frank speak. They both sense Janet has more to say.

Janet blows her nose and continues. "I've learned many harsh lessons during this awful time. We trusted everyone involved in managing the hostel from the volunteers to the manager." She almost spits the word 'manager'. "We've gone from trusting John Lincoln with the financial control, which essentially meant responsibility resting with one individual, to now getting dual, or even triple, authority on all transactions." Janet looks at Brian Carter.

Brian nods. "That's right. We've started to double check payment details sent by post with a phone call to confirm they're correct. Account details for payments must now be checked by a second person. Cash is proving particularly challenging to handle as you can imagine. Thinking of trying to ensure the collection and counting of cash donations is now witnessed and checked all the way to the bank. Such a move is tough in a relatively small charity like ours where we like to think of each other as friends as well as colleagues. "

Janet is nodding as he speaks. She adds, "Yes, those, like me, helping to organise things, left the finer details to Mr Lincoln. After all, he had been appointed as a highly experienced finance manager who knew what he was doing." Now she was sounding angry. " He even spent time supposedly redesigning our system to make it more efficient !" She laughs miserably. "You see, I feel responsible and really naive for accepting what I was told by him. I didn't check our bank accounts. I feel I should offer my resignation, but the trustees say no." She hangs her head and is quiet.

Brian tells her nobody blames her and she's not to worry.

Anna and Frank stay silent, waiting in case there is more to be revealed.

Suddenly, Janet looks up and says bitterly. "Would you believe that at an event recently, donors were handing £5, even £10, notes to guess who ! When he had a big bundle of notes in his hand, he held them up and joked: "I'm off on holiday now."

Janet looks close to tears. She sits quietly, looking down at the floor.

Frank nods to indicate the interview is at an end.

Anna finishes by saying, "thank you both for coming in. We realise how distressing this must be for you all. Please don't blame yourselves though. Con men like Lincoln are very clever at covering their tracks. It isn't your fault. You're both free to go now, although we shall probably need to speak to you again as the case progresses."

Janet and Brian stand up. Janet gives them a watery smile and the pair leave the room.

"Poor girl," observes Anna.

Frank nods.

---

(39) The Plot Thickens

"Learning never exhausts the mind."

Ben, alias Paul, has reported back with his progress. He's been praised for his efforts and encouraged to take the next step and meet with Harry, the man who lives underground, again.

Ben tells Frank Fernbank about Harry being an academic and historian, who became a drinker. He explains that Harry now acts as a kind of father figure to some of the younger homeless blokes. "There's a family of them living in the Underground shelter. The other old man I met at the hostel, Arthur, is respected throughout the homeless community and has become known as 'The Invisible Man' because he manages to move from place to place above ground, never staying on the same pitch, but still remaining in the locality around his home. He and Harry are old friends. Probably the same age, around sixty."

Frank Fernbank is 54 years old. He realises, of course, that to young officers like Ben, he is also 'old' !

Ben goes on to explain that Harry tells tales of how the current socio-political rulers now reject his academic contributions to the history of the country. As a result, he is obliged to 'hibernate' as he calls it.

As the discussion comes to an end, Frank Fernbank congratulates Ben on his good work. He doesn't want to overdo the praise though. Mustn't let the lad get complacent. Although Frank thinks this is unlikely in Ben's case.

That evening, Ben returns to continue his undercover work as Paul. On this occasion, he learns from Harry about using the underground shelters in WW2.

That night, Ben, as Paul, is sharing a meal with Harry in the Wood Green underground station.

"This station is one of many that were used as shelters during the war," begins Harry. Explore any of them and you'll discover a labyrinth of dark and dusty passageways which were once used by the travelling public. Here you've seen the well preserved vintage advertising poster fragments that have been concealed for years."

Paul nods.

Harry continues. "In the Autumn of 1940, Londoners made themselves like moles and went underground to avoid being killed by German bombs. I remember old Herbert Morrison, the Home Secretary, saying in 1944, 'We ought not to encourage a permanent day and night population underground. If that spirit gets abroad we are defeated.' He thought it smacked of defeatism you see."

Paul laughs at Harry's impersonation. He is interested though. He'd only been a toddler when the war ended, but now he finds snippets from older people's memories fascinating.

Harry continues. "While showing signs of defeatism was part of the worry, there was also a concern, among the powers that be, that an anti-authoritarian spirit might be bolstered ! Mind you, his fears weren't entirely without cause. There was a newsletter which circulated, denouncing the authorities as callous and neglectful of the people.

For this reason, sheltering in the tube wasn't an organised effort, it's just where Londoners went - and there was much discussion about whether or not it should be allowed to continue. Newspapers claimed that most of the people were not merely sheltering in the Tubes, they were actually living there. Probably better conditions than some of the slums in the East End," Harry adds cynically. Surprisingly, that said, many people did prefer to stay at home and take their chances sheltering in the pretty flimsy corrugated iron Anderson shelters in their gardens."

Paul nods. He's about to say he had an old Anderson shelter in his garden at home, then he quickly realised that would be a big boo boo !

"Anyhow," continues Harry, "people soon got their regular places to shelter and underground they set up little troglodyte communities where they could relax and feel safe. Some people even carried their treasured possessions down with them to their bunkers for safety !" Harry laughs. "Can you believe, I would occasionally give a hand to an old lady with a bursting suitcase in one hand and a bundle which appeared to contain all her cooking pots, ornaments, and her precious tea service in the other....Barmy. Quite barmy !"

Harry sits musing.

Paul tries to think of a way of getting more information without it sounding suspicious. "Do any of the blokes use that hostel place ? You know, 'Help the Homeless' ?

For a moment, Paul thinks that Harry won't say anything. Then, he's surprised at the heartfelt response.

"Not bloody likely if they've got any sense !"

"What d'you mean ?" asks Paul cautiously.

"Don't trust those do-gooders, " mumbles Harry.

"What d'you mean ?"

Harry leans over so that his face is closer to Paul's. "There's very suspicious things going on there if you want my opinion."

"Such as ?"

Harry looks around to ensure there are no eavesdroppers. The bloke that runs it.....he's well....crooked.....Oh there's no proof, but a number of us believe that he's robbing the place blind.....you know, cooking the books."

"Really !" Paul tries to sound surprised.

Harry pauses again. "There's also rumours that he's selling drugs to some of the blokes, 'specially the young ones."

This is news to Paul. The police suspect fraud, but drugs hadn't been mentioned as far as he knew.

"You use drugs ?" Harry asks suspiciously.

"No way. I'm never going down that path."

"Good lad. I've seen what they can do. Get the young ones started on cannabis, then pounce."

"What d'you mean ?"

"Heroin. Cocaine. Serious stuff."

"That's bad. Hasn't anyone reported it ?"

Harry looks at Paul, amazed. "Come on lad, you can't be that daft. Who's going to believe us old lags or young tearaways like yourself ?"

"Suppose so," says Paul, adopting a sulky tone.

"Listen....Paul, isn't it ? You go down the path of drugs and that's the way to a quick death.....or not so quick. The people that run these organisations are dangerous people. They think you're going to upset the apple cart, that could be a death warrant. No, my advice is keep schtum and keep away from that place, it's a magnet for trouble."

"S'ppose you're right."

"Believe me son, I am."

---

(40) Help the Homeless

"Time will inevitably uncover dishonesty and lies."

(Norodom Sihanouk)

Janet Gardner has been asked to come to the police station once more to explain the situation regarding progress in the investigation into the fraud. An official representing the Charity Commision, who can monitor charities' use of funds, a Mr Vernon Marsden, has been called in. He is an experienced accountant who has worked with the police in other such cases of fraud. The Woodstone team have been informed that he has been called in to examine the Help the Homeless' books and help unravel the complexities of the fraud and determine the final amounts of money missing. Ths evidence can then be presented in court when John Lincoln's case comes to trial.

Janet speaks to the team leaders DS Anna Kinsale, DI Roger Edwards and DCI Frank Fernbank. "It was a difficult time for everyone at the hostel, but Mr Marsden, the chief investigator, has been consistently reassuring. He has examined the cash flow figures and had to sort out the complicated ways in which John Lincoln had produced them so that, on the surface, everything seemed normal. Mr Marsden has constantly told us not to worry. He has taken charge of interpreting the incomings and outgoings. As you can imagine, it suits us to leave it to him because we were completly flumuxed. Mr Marsden's team of external accountants asked us whether we had managed to recoup any of the missing monies, such as the example of an invoice that, by chance, I had noticed Mr Lincoln had paid twice two years before. Remember, we found that Mr Lincoln had paid the second amount to himself by cheque, even using the forged signature of the previous Manager ! "

"Don't worry," says Anna. "The evidence that has been presented by the external accountants to the police and a police Fraud Team is irrefutable. The team of external accountants has immediately initiated an investigation on suspicion of gross misconduct."

Jannet continues to look miserable. " It's been a devastating experience for all of us, the staff , the volunteers and the trustees. Together with the Fraud team, we looked at every single transaction going back for all the years that Mr Lincoln was in charge. We found he had repeatedly stolen hundreds, even thousands, of pounds by writing cheques to himself. He had fabricated expenses and pocketed many of the cash donation s. Maureen and I had come to suspect that he had pilfered takings from many donation boxes and even envelopes which people had delivered directly to our door. We didn't have the proof though. Of course, as you know, once the cat was out of the bag, he was dismissed by the trustees and reported to the police."

Anna knows that the Fraud Squad had conducted lengthy interviews with the staff and volunteers at the hostel. Together with the external accountants they kept on digging. Now it had been revealed that there had been a history of cover-ups and mismanagement since John Lincoln had been in the job. The cashflow and the profit and loss figures he had been producing were rubbish. Cheques he claimed to have issued had never been sent ! It was a large, complicated muddle. Anna felt sorry for those like Janet and Maureen who had trusted John Lincoln implicitly.

Vernon Marsden explains that once all the evidence has been gathered, it will be presented to a solicitor. As soon as the culprit or culprits have been caught, the case will, eventually, come to court.

Janet had volunteered to write to key business donors in advance of the court hearing and newspaper coverage of the crime. She, like the others involved , are keen to not let them abandon the charity. To her relief, she tells us all they have, in the main, replied with sympathy. Sadly, some had often shared similar experiences.

Janet admits that she has learned many harsh lessons.. Now, the charity was going to be more tightly managed. Previous financial control, resting with one individual was now to be dual ,or even triple, monitored.

She continues. "We're starting to double check payment details from collection tins and those sent by post. Account details for payments are to be checked by a second person. Cash, of course, is particularly challenging to handle for a charity such as ours. We are trying to ensure that the collection and counting of cash donations are witnessed and checked all the way to the bank. That's hard, for quite a small charity such as ours. The trustees are going to appoint a highly experienced finance manager to initiate all these changes to our system." Janet pauses. " I still feel deeply upset. I feel partly responsible. I think I was naive for accepting what I was told, for not checking our bank accounts and for allowing such a sloppy system to continue.

I have offered to resign but, thankfully, the trustees wouldn't hear of it !" She smiles.

Frank Fernbank explains that his team had managed to arrest John Lincoln at the airport. Literally, only just before he was about to board a plane to Spain. Had he managed to get away, it would be unfortunate for the British courts because, according to Spanish law, extradition can only occur if the crime committed is a serious offence that is considered a crime in Spain as well. As the offence was not connected with murder or millions of pounds being stolen, it seems that, possibly, John Lincoln would not have been extradited to Britain any time soon.

Frank also mentions that there had been suggestions that Lincoln might return at least some of the money, but that seems highly unlikely as he did not seem the type of man who would have a guilty conscience !

---

(41) Murray Steps In

"Arriving at one goal is the starting point to another."

(John Dewey)

Anna and Roger are on their way to visit Stratford Police Station; only 3 miles away. The station is an old Victorian building. A stripe of bright sunlight crosses the facade. They enter, climbing the steep stone steps. Inside, the building is cool compared to outside. They head for the office of Detective Inspector Murray Jacobs.

Anna knocks on Murray's door and she and Roger enter.

Murray's face brightens. "Ah, The Lone Ranger and Tonto. Welcome friends ! " He grins. "Take a pew and I'll order us a cuppa."

Murray goes to the door and shouts "Bacon !"

Anna and Roger exchange puzzled glances. Moments later a young PC appears. Anna is pleased to see a male PC being asked to bring tea. Murray's learning !

While they wait for the tea, Anna begins. "Did you have any luck with Ted Merriman ?"

Murray nods. "Yes. As you know, he was the senior investigator at the time of O'Farrell's arrest.

Anna and Roger nod.

Murray continues. "I asked Ted if he could remember how O'Farrell reacted when he was arrested."

"Well," says Murray, " apparently, first impressions were that he was puzzled. Couldn't believe that we thought he'd done wrong."

Roger adds, "so he was angry, scared ?"

"No, as Ted emphasised, just puzzled. I reckon he thought he'd explain himself and we'd let him go. In Ted's opinion, he seemed like an innocent at that time. But we know how clever some crooks can be at hiding things, so we had to stick with him."

The others agree. The tea arrives.

Murray, takes a sip of his beverage, replaces the cup on the saucer, and muses for a moment. Ted says it's a case that always worried him. His instinct was, at the time, that he may well have been innocent, but it was presented as such an open and shut case. Trouble is now, you've been gathering evidence against O'Farrell's former boss which sounds pretty watertight."

"We have arrested John Lincoln," explains Roger. Although he's a suspect, he has to be found guilty before we can begin to think about overturning O'Farrell's sentence."

"If there has been a miscarriage of justice," says Anna, we need to try and get this sorted out as soon as possible…..I know from his sister that Patrick is in a very fragile state. He could even become suicidal."

Murray nods his head. "I have only been involved in one case where miscarriage of justice came to light." He shakes his head. "The trouble is it's very complicated and could take a lot of time. O'Farrell needs a lawyer who knows what he's doing."

Roger chips in. "I believe that guilty verdicts can be undone or annulled by a judge, at a Court of Appeal court when new evidence has been brought forward to prove that a so-called guilty person is, in fact, innocent. In O'Farrell's case that is John Lincoln's guilt."

Anna asks, "so, in the case of an appeal against the conviction, the Court, if they allow the appeal, has the power to quash the conviction ?"

Murray nods.

"But," adds Roger, looking at Anna's expectant face, "it can and most likely will, take time."

---

(42) Drugs!

"You can get the monkey off your back, but the circus never leaves town."

(Anne Lamott)

Anna and Roger arrive back at Woodstone to find DI Fernbank pacing up and down the office with a copy of The Daily Mirror' newspaper in his hands. He's staring at the headline on the front page and turning very red in the face.

As the pair enter, Fernbank turns to them waving the newspaper in their direction. "Have you seen this ?" he blusters.

Bothe shake their heads. Anna takes the newspaper and shares it with Roger. On the front page there is a headline which reads *"Makeshift 'crystal meth' lab discovered in tent hidden under bushes on The Flats."*

This is the area of Epping Forest which is on the territory of Woodstone Police Station.

"Bloody Drug Squad, bloody DI Moody, never even told me until this morning. Kept it quiet for security reasons. What the hell did he think we were going to do ? Warn the villains off ?"

There's an uncomfortable silence.

Anna knew, from the drugs course she had attended, that in the last few years, ever more substances were being made and therefore restricted in Britain, finally being banned in 1964. Crystal Meth, or to give it its proper name, Methamphetamine, had been used during World War Two. It had been issued to both British and American troops. It was used extensively to give greater stamina and tolerance to the psychological traumas of warfare to soldiers. After the war, production of methamphetamine began to go underground, and was increasingly used recreationally and known as 'crystal meth'.

Frank opens the newspaper and reads aloud. According to the newspaper account, "*the suspected drug-production 'tent' was said to be hidden under camouflage sheets, brambles and tree branches so that passers-by could not see the laboratory as people walked by. However, a dog walker got sight of the makeshift drug's 'cooking den' on The Flats on Tuesday and reported it to the police. Officers closed off the scene and erected a police tent to hide the laboratory where police specialists were now analysing the chemicals found in the tent-like structure. A source reportedly told this paper: 'The cooks on The Flats were trying to make crystal meth in a tent-like structure. They certainly had plenty of ventilation !'*

"They're taking the piss," says Frank. "The drug squad boys have been here, having a laugh at our expense !" He pauses, then throws the newspaper to the floor. "Making jokes about us country bumpkins not being able to find a drug den even when it's under our noses !"

"Let the tabloids have their fun," says Roger. "We've got John Lincoln and I'm sure he's got plenty more beans to spill !"

Anna reports to Frank what they have discovered from Murray's chat with Ted Merriman and a look at the file on the O'Farrell case.

"There's hope for O'Farrell that's true," says Frank," but Lincoln wasn't working alone. I've had plods looking for that garage boss…..Reg Houghton. His wife claims he hasn't been home for a couple of days. She has been shown a photo of John Lincoln and recognises him as an occasional visitor to the garage. I'm wondering now if Houghton is involved in the drugs game as well and has done a runner like Lincoln tried to do. Maybe they planned to meet up in Spain. Dumping the wives for some Spanish senoritas !"

Roger picks up on the disappearance of Reg Houghton. "Could he have left the country before Lincoln ? If he's been missing for several days, it could mean he's gone. Maybe they were going to travel on the same flight ?"

Frank looks at Anna. "It's a thought. Use the phone in your office and ring London Airport. See if anyone by the name of Reg Houghton has travelled on a plane to Spain in the last week."

Anna leaves the room. A short time later she returns. "Sorry, nobody of that name has taken a plane to anywhere in Spain in the last week."

"M'mm" responds Roger. He catches Anna's eye. "Remember when we tried to speak to him at the garage and he'd made up some story to his wife about going to see a car ?"

"Anna nods. Frank looks at her. "So that could mean he'd disappeared earlier than we thought. Go and have another word with Mrs Houghton. Find out exactly when she saw her husband."

Anna prepares to leave.

"Tell you what, Roger, let's go and have another go at Lincoln. See if anything crops up !"

---

(43) Where is Reg Houghton ?

Anna drives to Houghton's Garage. The premises are locked up and clearly unoccupied. She radios in and explains she is going over to the Houghton's home. The house is in a suburban location. The area seems quiet, even peaceful. She knocks on the door of the Houghton's red brick house. Mrs Houghton opens the door. She looks miserable and has clearly been weeping. Her eyes are red and she wipes them with a handkerchief before inviting Anna inside. The hallway, by contrast, is welcoming. On the walls are the framed photographs of two children smiling. The floor is an old-fashioned parquet, blending deep, homely shades of brown. The walls are the fresh greens of summer gardens. The place has the comforting feeling of warm woodland hues. This is in sharp contrast to the sorry figure of Margaret Houghton.

"I'm sorry if this is an inconvenient time," says Anna politely.

Mrs Houghton wipes her eyes. "No, that's all right dear. Come into the kitchen and I'll make us a nice cup of tea. "

Once the tea is made and the pair are sitting facing one another at the kitchen table, Anna begins. "I was hoping to have a word with Mr Houghton. I presume he's out at the moment ?"

Mrs Houghton is slow to respond. "No, he's not here at the moment dear." Tears reform in her eyes.

"Are you expecting him soon ?" Anna smiles at her reassuringly.

This question seems to elicit a sorry response. Margaret Houghton is feeling vulnerable. Her weeping begins in a quiet and desolate way.

"Tell me what's wrong ?" invites Anna politely.

"He's gone."

"What do you mean ?"

He's not been here for nearly a week. I've asked round. You know, spoken to his mates. No-one's seen him at all. He wouldn't just leave me. Leave the garage. It just doesn't make sense !"

Anna has an idea. Did you speak to Elsie or Fred Preston ?"

"I was reluctant at first. You know, with what happened to their Tom. Poor lad. But, neither of them had seen him......in fact, you may know Fred fell out with Reg."

Anna's ears prick up. "Really ?"

"Yes. I put it down to how heart-broken they were about poor Tom.....and the dreadful way he died."

Anna nods. "Was there any other reason for them falling out ?"

Mrs Houghton looks pensive. She hesitates. "Elsie, you know, his wife, told me Fred thought Reg was up to something..... I mean something dodgy. Fred's an honest bloke and I think he suspected Reg of something bad.....but I don't know what."

"Do you have any reason to believe your husband was up to anything ?"

Mrs Houghton hesitates. "Well, Fred came here one afternoon. He'd tried to get Reg at the garage, but nobody was there, I told him that Reg had gone off on business somewhere. Said he'd be back late.....Fred seemed....I dunno....annoyed."

Anna nods and stays quiet, hoping Mrs Houghton will elaborate.

"I don't know. It might be something to do with that Tony chap. I haven't seen him for ages. Reg took him on and as far as I know he was a good mechanic. Then, he seemed to just disappear off the scene."

"M'mm. Could Reg and Tony have been up to something ?"

"Like what ?" asks Mrs Houghton, looking puzzled.

Anna decides to jump in at the deep end. "Could your husband and Tony Blake have been involved in some kind of unlawful activity ?"

"Thieving you mean ?"

"No, I mean drugs."

"Drugs !" Mrs Houghton looks horrified. "No. No. Surely not !"

"I'm sorry, Margaret. I know that idea must upset you, but it could be that Reg got involved without realising what he was getting into." Anna doesn't believe this for one moment, but she wants to keep Margaret Houghton on side.

Margaret sits quietly, studying her handkerchief, as if it could hold the answer to the mystery of her husband's disappearance.

Anna decides to leave things there. She stands up. "Look Margaret, if Reg gets back, please tell him to contact the police station. Maybe we've got the wrong end of the stick, but we must speak to him."

Margaret nods and shows Anna to the door. Anna momentarily places her hand on Margaret's arm. "Let's hope we can get the mystery solved as soon as possible."

Margaret gives a wary smile and closes the door behind Anna.

---

(44) Talking it Through

"All human interactions are opportunities either to learn or to teach."

(Scott Peck)

Anna finally arrives back at the station in the early evening after a busy day. Her mind working nineteen to the dozen about the apparent disappearance of Reg Houghton.

She decides she has to go back to the nick after speaking to Margaret Houghton. Once there, she telephones London Airport departures to see if anyone of that name had booked a flight to anywhere. Maybe Houghton wasn't going to Spain. She asked about a Reginald Houghton going anywhere else, but it seemed there was no record of anyone by that name leaving the country in the last ten days.

She has to discuss it with Frank and Roger. They both reckon that Houghton is hiding out somewhere. Where though ?

Frank suggests getting Houghton's call details from Post Office Telecommunications, from both his work and home telephone lines. Anna takes charge of this task. Roger is charged with the task of contacting Fred Preston to see if he knows anything. Tony Blake and John Lincoln are both in custody and Frank Fernbank is to interview them again and see if he can find out about their relationships with Houghton.

It's going to be a late leaving time. Anna had planned to go for a pub meal with Murray, so she phones him to let him know. After explaining things to him, Anna is surprised when Murray reveals some information which could possibly explain Reg Houghton's disappearance.

Murray says, "that's a strange one. As it happens, just today, we have a case of an unidentified male body."

Anna 's heart skips a beat. "Where was this ?"

"In a warehouse under the railway arches at Bethnal Green. Shot straight through the heart. Probably some dodgy dealing gone wrong."

"Have you got a description of the man ?"

Murray looks puzzled. "Why ?"

"We have a man involved in a drugs and murder case gone missing."

"Hang on. I'll get one of the PCs who found him."

Murray calls the desk sergeant.

"The constable is having a bite to eat in the canteen." he's told.

"Can you get him to my office pronto ?"

"Yes sir."

Shortly afterwards there is a knock on Murray's door. A young constable appears.

"Yes Sir ?"

"I understand you discovered a body in one of the warehouses under the arches."

"Yes sir."

"Any idea how long he'd been there ?"

"A bit whiffy sir. Maybe a week or more ?"

"M'mm. Can you give me a description ?"

"Middle-aged. Dark hair. Wearing a brown suit."

"Cause of death ?"

"Bullet right through the heart, sir. Reckon the killer knew what he was doing."

Anna listens spellbound.

Murray picks up and explains this to Anna. "Sound familiar ?"

"Could be," says Anna.

"The body's at the mortuary,...er....Sergeant," explains the PC.

Murray again speaks to Anna and she responds. "I have a car outside. I know where the mortuary is."

The constable then takes his leave.

"Want me to accompany you, Sergeant ?" Murray grins.

Anna laughs. "No, I'll manage, thank you, Detective Inspector." She hangs up the telephone.

Anna returns to her car and sets off. Ten minutes later she arrives at the mortuary.

The mortuary is only a short drive from the Police Station. The area comprises what had once been middle-class homes and public buildings of the Victorian era. The architectural features of the mortuary building comprise a red brick construction under an elaborate roof line. When Anna arrives inside she follows a dimly lit corridor until she discovers a room on the left with a nameplate reading 'Mortuary'. She opens the door. The room has white tiles on the walls and a chilly atmosphere which gives Anna the shivers.

A woman looks up and smiles. "Hello. Can I help you ?"

Anna can't help thinking that the woman's friendly greeting is in contrast to the cold, unwelcoming surroundings.

Anna produces her ID card. "Detective Sergeant Anna Kinsale."

The young woman dries her hands and walks over to shake hands with Anna.

Anna explains that she would like to see the body of the unknown man brought in recently.

The Mortician appears and his co-worker tells him what Anna needs to do.

"Strange case," muses the Mortician. "Looks well-dressed, but no ID found on the body."

Anna explains that the body may be a missing man they are looking for.

The man accompanies her to an adjacent room where there is a large metal locker unit housing a number of doors with handles. Opened up, each one reveals a body lying on a shelf which can be pulled out to reveal the dead person. The Mortician pulls one such handle and the body is exposed. As soon as Anna sees him she knows it is indeed Reg Houghton.

"The Doc says bullet through the heart. Gunman knew what he was doing. Apparently a semi-automatic pistol. No doubt. The Doc thought it could be a German Luger. Lots of them have turned up in criminal hands since the war. " He goes on to explain. "It's a handgun that automatically ejects and loads cartridges in its chamber after every shot fired. Only one round of ammunition is fired each time the trigger is pulled. Quick and easy. Perfect for gangsters bumping off their enemies."

"Really. So that's the weapon we're looking for ?"

"Most likely, going by the Doc's opinions."

Anna leaves and makes her way back to the station. Once there she goes straight to Frank Fernbank's office. He smiles. "Thought I'd wait and see how you got on."

Anna gives the news.

"Well now, the plot thickens," grins Frank. I've been interviewing John Lincoln. Remember when background checks were done on the man a while ago. Turns out that he was an officer during the war, a Captain and, here's the best bit, Reg Houghton was his batman !"

"Wow !" So that ties up with the gun then ?"

"Yes, but Lincoln's house was thoroughly searched after his arrest, so that gun's whereabouts is unknown."

"Wouldn't he have disposed of it after killing Houghton ?"

"Yes. It could be at the bottom of the Thames as far as we know. However, I'm now going to order another search of Lincoln's home and his office at 'Help the Homeless." He smiles at Anna and hesitates. "Good work, Sergeant !"

---

(45) A Release for Patrick ?

"Bad news travels fast. Good news takes the scenic route."

— Doug Larson

Anna has agreed to help Philomena to investigate the possibility of an early release from prison for her brother Patrick. Anna and Philomena have spoken to the lawyer, Peter Wilkins, who defended Patrick during his original time in court. She has discovered from him that, according to the law, if an inmate in prison believes they were wrongfully convicted of a crime they did not commit, they may have the opportunity to prove their innocence and be released early. However, he has warned, the process of proving innocence and obtaining early release can be complex and challenging.

Peter has suggested one possible avenue for proving Patrick's innocence is through a legal appeal or a petition for post-conviction relief. Patrick himself, or his legal representative, would need to identify new evidence that was not presented at the original trial, such as eyewitness testimony, or other facts that cast doubt on the conviction. In Lincoln's case, there is now sufficient evidence, both from the trustees, employees and volunteers of the Help the Homeless charity. There is also now evidence of Lincoln's guilt via physical evidence of theft of money from the charity's funds. All this proof of evidence would need to be presented to the court and proven to be credible and convincing. If the court finds that the evidence is sufficient to undermine the original conviction, the inmate may be granted a new trial or may be released from prison at once.

Peter has suggested that another option is to seek a pardon or clemency via the prison governor. A pardon would be an official forgiveness for the crime and could result in Patrick's release from prison. However, Peter has warned that such pardons are typically granted only in exceptional circumstances and require a showing of evidence of innocence or other compelling factors, such as the admission of guilt by the real culprit. In this case, John Lincoln. Although Lincoln is in custody, this would mean a confession and/or provision of compelling evidence from the police investigation.

"This latter might be a quicker option," suggests Peter, "considering the real culprit is in custody and the evidence is there."

"Would you help him ?" asks Philomena nervously.

"I certainly would. It's worth noting though that it might also be a lengthy and difficult process. Even if Patrick is able to prove his innocence, a worst case scenario might be that he might not be automatically entitled to early release, bearing in mind that there may be other legal requirements or procedural hurdles that need to be overcome. Don't underestimate the time span. I certainly think Patrick has the evidence we need to put together a case, but be aware it can be a challenging and uncertain process.

Philomena looks worried and nervous.

"Don't worry," says Peter. "I'll do my very best for him. In fact,", he looks at Anna, "I'll speak to your boss, as I know you've kept him informed about what's going on and he's got plenty of evidence against John Lincoln even if he won't confess."

Peter smiles at Philomena. "I'll get in to see Patrick as quickly as I can. Why don't you go on the next visiting day and tell him the good news ? I'm sure that will help his mental state."

Philomena and Anna get up to leave. Philomena thanks Peter profusely.

"I can't wait to see Patrick. Thanks so much for your help and your belief in Patrick's innocence."

Anna beams and the two women return to their flat with arms linked.

---

(46) John Lincoln and Reg Houghton

DCI Frank Fernbank has invited Anna to be his partner in the investigative interview with John Lincoln. It will be her first time to be involved in the interviewing of a potential murderer.

Frank Fernbank gives her advice. "Prior to going through the process and stages of investigative interviewing, it's essential that you first appreciate and accept what we call the golden rule of interviewing. It is a simple rule to understand but you have to make sure that you apply the rules at all times in your professional practice. We all may have gut instinct, but if we don't stick to the rules then we might lose a case, if it was visited at a later date. Nobody should be able to say that we didn't give Lincoln a fair chance to respond. However much it may gall you, play it straight if you want to become a skilful police investigative interviewer!"

Anna nods.

"Another thing to remember," explains Frank, "is the difference between Interviewing and interrogating." You've been involved in a number of interviews, but interrogation is what we'll use in the case of John Lincoln. He's been interviewed already, but now we're possibly talking murder as well as serious fraud and drug dealing. That means a harsher approach. That said, we are still required to demonstrate the same professional standards of impartiality and treat the bugger with respect and dignity throughout !"

Anna grins her understanding.

"Remember, " adds Frank, "our goal is obtaining an admission of guilt. I think getting a confession will be difficult, if not impossible. However, when his case gets to court, it will be fully substantiated by all the strong information and evidence we've gathered. Remember that this will enable us to present a better case against Lincoln."

Frank and Anna walk to the interview room. Moments later, John Lincoln is brought in by an accompanying PC. Following them is Lincoln's lawyer, Brian Garnett.

Frank begins by cautioning Lincoln. " You do not have to say anything. But it may harm your defence if you do not mention when questioned something which you later rely on in court. Anything you do say may be given in evidence."

"No comment", says Lincoln, an arrogant expression on his face.

Anna assumes that this standard response was probably advised by Lincoln's lawyer in the light of compelling police evidence. If he continues to do this, however, it will probably do him more harm than good.

Nevertheless, Anna feels extremely frustrated. To be confronted with this smirking man who seems to think he's above the law, is galling.

As the interview continues, Lincoln continues to say nothing, or at best, 'no comment'. It's infuriating because he uses tactics like closing his eyes, whilst being questioned. At this present moment he is staring at a fixed point beyond the heads of the two police officers. Each question elicits actions such as trying to turn his chair or, at least, his body, away from his interviewers. This enables him to avoid eye contact altogether.

Anna sees that her boss is not going to be cowed by this behaviour.

DCI Fernbank continues. "Do you own a gun, Mr Lincoln ?"

This question elicits a response. "Not since the war. No."

"Ah. The war. I understand from your military record that you were responsible for the capture and detention of a group of German soldiers on D-Day ?"

"That's correct," smirks Lincoln. "I was awarded the DSO."

"Admirable," responds Fernbank.

"Could it be that you took and retained a Luger pistol from one of these soldiers ?"

"They would have been disarmed and the weapons disposed of in the correct manner."

"That doesn't answer my question, Mr Lincoln."

John Lincoln raises his eyebrows. "That's all I have to say on the matter."

Fernbank remains calm. "Do you know a man by the name of Reginald Houghton ?"

Lincoln touches his forehead with his hand in an exaggerated fashion and a puzzled expression on his face. "No, I don't believe I do."

Anna sees a smirk creeping onto her boss's face.

"That's odd, sir. He was your batman during the war."

"My batman ?.......Oh yes, you mean old Howie !.......Haven't seen him for donkey's years."

"Really ? You were witnessed recently having an argument with the man at his place of work by Mrs Houghton who works in the office there !"

"Ah yes. I'd forgotten that….tried to put a bit of business his way some time back by buying a Jag from him. Damn thing never ran well. The bugger diddled me….." Lincoln smiles charmingly at Anna. "Oh sorry. Ladies present."

Anna remains stoney-faced. There's a pause in the proceedings before the interview begins again. Then, there's a knock on the door.

Fernbank looks at Anna and she opens the door and steps into the corridor. There's WPC Lily Saunders waiting there with a grin on her face.

"The gun's been found," she announces to Anna. " Hidden under the spare tyre in the boot of his car can you believe ! He'd left the car at the airport before he was arrested !"

Anna smiles. "Too clever for his own good, that one," she says. "Thanks Lily."

Anna returns to the interview room. After sitting down, she writes a note on the pad in front of her and hands it to Frank Fernbank. She senses his reaction, which he hides well.

He then speaks to John Lincoln. "A Luger gun has been found in the boot of your car in the airport car park. Do you have anything to say ?"

Lincoln looks at his lawyer. Brian Garnett. He speaks to DCI Fernbank. "May we halt the interview here please. I should like to speak to my client alone."

"Of course," replies DCI Fernbank. "In the meantime we shall be dusting the gun for fingerprints."

For the first time in the interview, apprehension appears on Lincoln's facial expression. His fingerprints had been taken after he had been arrested and taken back to the police station.

Back in the office, Fernbank advises Anna that the fingerprints are a good sign of proof, but the link with the drug-dealing has also to be proven to tie in with a reason for John Lincoln murdering Reg Houghton.

(47) Fred Preston Chips In

"Focus on the step in front of you, not the whole staircase."

PC Lily Saunders knocks on the door of Frank Fernbank's office.

"Come" is the response.

She steps in and advises Frank that Fred Preston, the father of the murdered lad, Tom Preston, has arrived at the station asking to see DCI Fernbank.

"Show him up."

As Lily departs, Frank rubs his hands together in anticipation.

Fred Preston arrives, accompanied by PC Saunders. Frank nods at Lily and she leaves the room.

Frank shakes Preston's hand and invites him to "Take a seat."

Fred Preston sits down opposite Frank who waits patiently while the other man gathers his thoughts. Frank studies his face. Heartbreak is written deep on the man's face. Frank has an adult son himself and cannot begin to think about the pain and stress of the loss of a child on both brain and body.

Tom's death must be made worse by the knowledge that he was murdered in such a horrific manner.

Fred Preston begins to speak. "I've been doing some investigating of my own. I found out that Reg Houghton is one of the regulars at The Blue Boar in Stapleford. Apparently, one of his drinking pals is a nasty bloke by the name of Dave Johnson."

DCI Fernbank's brain goes into overdrive. "New one on me. Do you think he might be involved in Tom's death ?"

"Well, the thing is that he's got a dog."

Fernbank's instincts are sharpened by this new name and the news of a dog."

Fred Preston leans forward. "Apparently this dog has been trained to be aggressive. Johnson uses it as a guard dog for his garage and scrapyard. It's known to have attacked, even bitten, people visiting the yard, even though some are bona fide customers."

Fernbank picks up his pen and jots notes on his pad. "Where is this scrapyard ?"

"Apparently, it's somewhere near Salcott on the Essex Marshes. Pretty remote spot by all accounts."

Fernbank's heart skips a beat. Large, fierce dog, trained to attack. It made perfect sense.

"I had thought of going down there. You know suss him out, but I think I'd get a pretty confrontational greeting. It's why I'm here."

"You've done the right thing, Mr Preston. It's the first we've heard of this character. Obviously keeps a low profile. I can't promise you anything at this point, but be assured we will check this information out thoroughly."

"Will you keep me posted ?" Fred Preston is both anxious and hopeful.

"Indeed we will. If you think of anything that might be helpful, even something small, don't hesitate to get in touch."

Fred Preston gives a troubled look. "I will."

Fernbank accompanies Fred Preston to the exit and then makes his way to Anna and Roger's room. Anna isn't there, but DI Roger Edwards is sitting at his desk going through his notes.

"Got some news for you, Roger."

"Oh ?"

Frank explains his conversation with Fred Preston. "I'd like you and Anna to go down to Salcott and find a garage and scrapyard."

"Salcott ? On the marshes ? A few minutes pass while Roger racks his brains. "Yes, I've got it. When Anna and I went to the garage to speak to Reg Houghton, he wasn't there, but his wife said he'd gone to a garage to look at a car. She didn't know where it was, but maybe it was at Salcott ?"

The two men smile meaningfully at one another. Frank explains that the owner is a man named Dave Johnson. "The interesting news is that he has a vicous dog which has been known to attack visitors to the site. So, what if ? ………."

Roger looks at his watch. "Anna's back anytime soon. I'll wait for her and then we'll head off to Salcott straight away !"

"Good. Let's live in hope !"

Shortly after Frank has returned to his office, Anna appears. Roger puts her in the picture. She listens carefully and then announces excitedly . "What are we waiting for ? Let's go."

It's a thirty minute drive to Salcott. The premises are to be found outside the village. A collection of old, scruffy buildings, including a couple of wartime nissen huts sit on a site which is muddy and untidy. Rusting car parts lie dumped in heaps. Old cars are piled on top of each other awaiting the crusher. Roger and Anna both knew that since the MOT had been introduced in 1960, it had proved to be the day of reckoning for old wrecks. People had started dumping their old cars en masse, rather than paying for repairs needed to pass MOT. The glut of old cars was more than the used car system could handle, and even massive numbers of largely functional cars, in more or less decent condition, ended up going to junkyards. Worse still the police were always being called to arrange the movement of discarded cars from roadsides and field entrances. Trouble was, the volume was more than junkyards could handle, also, rather than keep cars around and try to sell parts off them, they had to be scrapped right away to make room for the constant flow of new arrivals. Hence the use of car crushers !

Arriving at the scrapyard in Salcott, the whole place seems derelict and depressing. Close to the entrance is a dilapidated caravan. Roger parks the police car close to the entrance and the caravan to avoid stepping into the oozing sludge. A plank has been placed across the mire as a pathway to the caravan. An untidy notice attached to the door of the caravan reads "Beware of the dog." At first, there is no sign of the dog. As they approach the caravan, a large Alsation inside the van leaps up at the window closest to the pair and begins barking loudly and scratching the side of the van, clearly keen to get outside and attack its prey.

Moments later a man approaches them with a stern expression on his face. He stomps his way towards them in a filthy overall and muddy gum boots. It's clear that he has noticed the police car and is ready for an aggressive confrontation. He stops a few feet from them.

"What d'you want, copper ?" He addresses Roger whilst looking sneeringly at Anna. "Bringing girls to back you up now ?"

Roger ignores his manner. "We just need to have a word, Mr Johnson."

"Well, you can have it right here."

"I believe you know a Reg Houghton ?"

"So," is the curt reply.

"Unfortunately, Mr Houghton has been found dead in suspicious circumstances."

"What's that got to do with me ?"

"Do you own a gun Mr Johnson?"

"No."

"Were you in the armed forces during the war ?"

"So."

"Did you ever bring any weapons back with you as souvenirs ?"

"No. Look mate, I never done Reg in. Why would I want to ? Him and me did a fair bit of business so why would I want him dead ?"

"Anna suddenly chips in. "Do you remember a young chap who worked for Reg ? Tom Preston was his name."

"Might have seen him there on occasions. He never come here though." Anna and Roger study Johnson's body language carefully. It's clear he seems a bit nervous despite his responses.

Roger takes a step forward. "Perhaps we could step into your caravan and discuss the matter further."

Johnson sighs and steps towards the caravan. "I better put Fang on his leash. He might be a bit partial to a copper's legs ! "

Roger and Anna step back a little.

Suddenly, without warning, Johnson pulls open the door of the caravan and Fang leaps out.

Both officers have received training for such circumstances. They know to avoid eye contact with the animal.

"Call the dog off," instructs Roger.

Johnson's response is to cross his arms. An unpleasant smile appears on his lips.

"Turn your body slowly to the side and cross your arms", whispers Roger to Anna.

Anna knows to completely ignore the dog. The dog comes to a halt, not sure of its next move. Luckily Roger has left the car doors open. They both stand still whilst the dog comes to a halt, surprised that its prey hasn't run away. It eyes them suspiciously. They both back up along the plank.

"You go for the back seat. Act slowly. I'll get in the driver's side."

They back away slowly. Fortunately for them the dog stops, probably puzzled at the behaviour of its potential prey. They both turn slightly and each slowly opens their respective car doors. As soon as they are comfortably seated they each quickly close the car doors. That's a signal for the aptly named Fang to take a leap at the car.

Roger starts the car up and slowly turns the wheel so that they are facing the exit from the muddy yard. Meantime, Johnson races to a car parked a few yards away, frantically turns the wheel and shoots past the police car, churning up the oozing brown slush on the ground.

The dog looks confused and returns to the safety of the caravan.

Anna jumps out of the car and takes the front passenger seat. Johnson accelerates wildly into the narrow country lane, turning right towards the main road. Roger follows, police siren blaring. Anna gets onto the police radio and asks for other police cars to intervene and set up a road block further along the main road. By the time Roger reaches the road block, it is clear that Johnson has stopped his car just before the road block and taken off on foot along the edge of a field. An officer on foot is chasing after him. Roger instructs the other driver to follow and assist his colleague. Anna and Roger wait anxiously by their car. Shortly afterwards, Johnson is led back in handcuffs, accompanied by the two police officers. Roger reads him his rights, making clear that he is being arrested in connection with the death of Tom Preston and possible involvement in the death of Reginald Houghton.

Johnson looks down at his feet and fails to make eye contact with any of the police officers. He remains silent.

Roger instructs the driver of the police car to take the handcuffed man to Woodstone nick. Anna is to accompany them. In the meantime, Roger radios for assistance with catching and controlling the dog, Fang. He will wait for the especially trained dog handler and the police vet to arrive before he follows the others to the police station.

Upon arrival at Woodstone police station, Anna accompanies one of the officers to an interview room, along with the handcuffed Dave Johnson. She calls DCI Frank Fernbank to conduct the interview with her.

Frank Fernbank opens the proceedings. "You do not have to say anything, but it may harm your defence if you do not mention when questioned anything you later rely on in court."

Despite this being a warning of the consequences of not answering questions, Johnson refuses to look at them or say anything. He is removed to a cell.

---

(48) Tying Up Loose Ends

"Stories don't like to end when you want them to, do they? Loose ends aren't easy to snip with scissors or tuck inside a hem. They tempt you. They want you to keep pulling until there is nothing left to keep you warm."

(Jan Ellison, A Small Indiscretion)

Anna is pleased to have tied up the loose ends. There are still court cases to come and verdicts to be decided. Looking back on the work she has been involved in over the past 3 months, it seems as if the whole business had been a storm. She's come through it. Learned lessons and gained experience. Now it's over, she thinks about how she had managed to survive. She thinks that one thing is sure. Having survived this storm, she will never be the same person who stepped into it at the start. That's what being a police officer is all about. Anna wonders how long it will be until the next storm starts brewing. For now, she's off to the pub with her fellow officers to celebrate.

Printed in Great Britain
by Amazon